DRIVEN

DJINN DOMINION: BOOK 3

CHRISTINE POPE

DARK VALENTINE PRESS

DRIVEN

ISBN: 978-1-946435-16-3

Copyright © 2018 by Christine Pope

Published by Dark Valentine Press

Cover design by Lou Harper

Print formatting by Indie Author Services

ONE

Bailey O'Keefe took the corner of Third Street and Flower at exactly forty-two miles per hour, rubber burning, smoke billowing from the tires of the Porsche 911 she was driving. A quick glance in the rearview mirror told her that the djinn currently in hot pursuit was about thirty yards behind her, and fading fast.

Good.

As soon as she hit the straightaway, Bailey mashed her foot down on the accelerator, and the car leapt forward, leaving the djinn who'd been following her even farther behind in her dust. However, she could still see him there, a grimly determined figure in fluttering dark blue robes, shooting like an arrow down Flower Street. At any other time in the world's history, this might have been an incongruous sight at best, since in general you didn't see someone in vaguely Middle Eastern clothing flying through downtown Los Angeles—unless a film crew happened to be shooting a movie nearby. By this point, however, more than six months after the Heat wiped out humanity and the djinn had taken over, those airborne elementals were almost commonplace.

The intersection with Sixth Street was coming up. Bailey took a hard left, still staying above forty miles an hour, and risked another glance in the rearview mirror. No sign of the djinn, and a grim smile touched her lips.

Time to go to ground.

The high-rise coming up on her left concealed one of her numerous hiding places. She turned down the steeply sloped driveway, slowing so she wouldn't scrape the car's ground effects on the cement, and disappeared into the parking garage. During the months she'd been using downtown L.A. as her home base, she'd created a network of these hidey-holes, underground garages where she'd lifted the entrance gates or pulled the barriers out of the way so she could gain entry. Too bad the power was out, because it would've been a lot easier if she could have just gotten the remotes for these various gates from vehicles abandoned in the area and then let those gates shut behind her, offering another layer of protection.

Unfortunately, life was rarely easy in this post-Heat world.

So far, none of the djinn had tracked Bailey to any of her hideouts. She always made sure her supernatural pursuers were safely out of eyeshot before she pulled into a garage, and she'd meticulously gone around the downtown area and opened as many of these barriers as she could find in order to conceal which places she actually used on a regular basis. Each hideout contained a bug-out bag stocked with bottled water, freeze-dried trail food, a change of underwear, and a bedroll. The accommodations might not have been the most luxurious, but they'd kept her safe and alive during the past seven months, despite her otherworldly stalkers.

This particular djinn, though—he was tenacious. Until he'd appeared on the scene, she'd noticed that all of the djinn who pursued her gave up after a few days. They were interested in an easy hunt, and she had determined that capturing her would be anything but easy for the bastards. But this one…he'd been stalking her for almost a week now and showed no signs of giving up. Good thing she knew this territory like the back of her hand. He could chase her all he wanted, but he'd never be able to actually catch her.

Bailey parked the Porsche in a far corner of the lowest level of the garage, making sure it was mostly concealed behind a support pillar. There might have been faster cars in L.A., but the Porsche suited her just fine, since it sat on corners like nobody's business and wasn't too much of a gas hog. Its bright turquoise color wasn't exactly discreet, but since the 911 was the only car currently operating in the downtown Los Angeles area—or probably anywhere else in the world—the color didn't really matter. It attracted attention simply because of what it was.

If she'd still been with the group of survivors who'd hidden in the steam tunnels underneath the Caltech campus right after the Heat struck, one of them might have pointed their finger at her and said, "I told you so," since they'd been convinced that attempting to drive rather than going everywhere on foot was the fastest way to attract the djinns' attention. But everyone in that group was now dead, or at least, Bailey assumed they were. No one else seemed to live and move in L.A., and although the group had done pretty well during those first terrible weeks after the Heat destroyed most of humanity, she had thought they were making a fatal error by stubbornly refusing to use any abandoned cars to shuttle them from hiding place to hiding place. True, cars could be loud, and the djinn would of course notice any kind of vehicle traffic when most of the world was dead. However, after observing a couple of djinn attacks, watching how they worked, she'd made a significant discovery.

Even the djinn who could fly through the air —as opposed to blinking themselves from place to place—didn't seem able to go any faster than forty miles an hour. She'd clocked them, marking how long it took them to move from intersection to intersection, a skill she'd picked up back in her old street racing days. At first she hadn't wanted to believe, because it seemed like such an obvious weakness, but further observation proved her hypothesis to be true.

And well, forty miles an hour was a pretty piddling number, especially with the kind of cars Bailey was used to driving.

After she'd left the Caltech group, she hiked most of the way from Pasadena to downtown Los Angeles, mainly because the streets in between— and the curving 110 Freeway—were filled with vehicles abandoned wherever they'd been when their drivers succumbed to the deadly fever that took out most of the world's population. When she'd gotten to the outskirts of downtown, though, she saw that most of the cars had been moved out of the way, that they were either gone entirely, or had been carefully set alongside the curb so the streets were clear.

The djinn had to have emptied the streets. Why, she had no idea, but she wasn't about to look a gift horse in the mouth. She'd taken a brand-new Camaro, wiped the dust of its former owner off the driver's seat, and headed for the maze of streets at the city's center, figuring that would be the best place to hide out, with all the myriad hidey holes downtown offered.

Bailey hadn't been there for more than twenty minutes before the first djinn appeared, forcing her to put her hypothesis to the test. Sure enough, he couldn't keep up with her, although she realized soon enough that the Camaro, while flashy, didn't hunker down enough on the turns to satisfy her requirements. A few days of searching through downtown L.A.'s parking garages had turned up the Porsche, which was so new, it still had paper dealer plates and less than a hundred miles on the odometer. No need to hot-wire it, because the key fob had been safely stowed at the valet station at the Biltmore Hotel.

God, she loved that car.

Sometimes she wondered whether it was wrong to get so much enjoyment out of driving the 911 and evading her djinn pursuers when so many people had died. Then again, nothing she did now was going to bring any of those people back. Maybe one day one of those djinn would catch up with her, and then she'd be just as dead as everyone else. In the meantime, she might as well indulge herself by giving them the middle finger whenever she could.

She got a camping lantern out of the Porsche's trunk and brought it over to where her bug-out bag was located, then spread the bedroll on the ground and sat down. It was very dark in here, except for the small circle of light the lantern provided, but Bailey refused to be spooked by the darkness, the way it seemed to press in on her. There was nothing to be afraid of in these underground shelters, except maybe some rats. Even they hadn't seemed too interested in her the few times she'd come across them. They'd been fat and sassy, glossy and healthy, and she wondered where they were getting food to eat. After all, this wasn't the sort of messy apocalypse that left a lot of corpses around for the rats to feed on. No, all the dead had disappeared into nice, neat piles of dust, no clean-up required. Kind of handy, actually.

As Bailey got a protein bar out of her bag, she thought about the djinn who'd once again pursued her today. Even though she'd managed to give him the slip this afternoon, his persistence worried her a bit. He'd first come on the scene about a week ago, had scared the shit out of her when he popped into existence out of nowhere while she was plundering the contents of a bodega down near some fancy lofts over by downtown's Arts District. Instinct had taken over, and she'd run to the Porsche, flung her swag onto the passenger seat, and zoomed out of there at almost a hundred miles an hour. He'd given pursuit, but there was no way he could fly fast enough to keep up, and she'd lost him soon enough.

But he hadn't given up. It seemed as though almost every time she came up from one of her underground lairs, he was waiting for her, although never close enough to make her worry that he actually knew where she'd been hiding. No, he was just one lucky son of a bitch.

Not lucky enough, though, considering she'd just given him the slip again.

She chewed on her protein bar, considering her nameless pursuer. Unlike the other djinn who'd given chase over the last six months, who all seemed dark and somewhat Mediterranean in appearance, this djinn had sandy hair and fair skin tanned to a light golden brown. He'd never gotten close enough for her to see what color his eyes were—thank God—but she got the feeling they were probably blue. Like all djinn, he seemed physically perfect in appearance, with the kind of abs a gym rat would kill for and bulging biceps revealed by the sleeveless, open robe he wore. If she'd seen him at a club or at street race, she probably would have gone up and flirted with him. Problem was, this djinn wasn't looking for a hook-up.

No, he only wanted to make sure she was dead, just like every other human being on the face of the planet.

Too bad. If he was going to be successful, he would have to do a lot better than he had today. And that didn't seem very likely, considering she had the laws of physics on her side.

Smiling, she reached for the bottle of water, took a swig, and began mentally planning for another day of pursuit.

———

Nasim al-Jibril lowered himself to the pavement and stood in the middle of the street, arms crossed, a scowl creasing his brow. There hadn't been any real reason for him to believe that he would best the woman today, not when she had already defeated him five times this week, but hope, it seemed, sprang eternal.

That vehicle she drove was so damnably fast.

Still frowning, he walked a few paces and then paused so he could look around at the buildings that towered above him. Many of those structures had underground parking facilities; he assumed that was where she managed to keep hiding herself. Perhaps he should undertake an organized inspection of them to see if he could turn up any trace of her, but the problem was, there were so very many, she would most likely have moved on to the next by the time he caught up with her. As far as he could tell, she had no plan of action when she drove, except to evade him, and so her erratic movements made it doubly difficult to determine where she might have gone to ground.

It had taken a while for the rumors about this ghost of a woman who haunted the streets of downtown Los Angeles to reach Nasim's ears. The lands he had been given for his own were far north of here, in a place men had once called Napa, and so many months had passed before he heard of her, in tales traded by those who had made it their duty to rid the world of mankind's last remnants, those miserable survivors who had somehow been immune to the fever the djinn had created. But as soon as he learned of her, the flaxen-haired woman in a car the color of the sky, he'd determined to come to L.A. and see if he would have any better luck than those who'd pursued her in the past.

Not that he had any true stomach for killing. He had not been among the reavers, the ones who took joy in eradicating humanity from this world. However, this woman presented a challenge, and Nasim felt he could sorely use a challenge. The place he had settled was very beautiful, true, but there was not a great deal to occupy him there, especially since the grapevines had been just past harvest when he arrived to inspect his new home. Before he had been given his lands, he had only thought of wine in terms of how much he enjoyed drinking it, but now he realized he would need to care for the vines if they were to survive. He had read books on the subject and pruned here and there as needed, had kept away the frost and made sure no harmful insects would attack the fragile plants, but there was not much else to do until the fruit appeared on the vines. It seemed the perfect time to travel here and see if he could catch this woman who had escaped so many others of his kind.

What he hadn't expected was her beauty. She appeared quite young, no more than twenty-five human years at the most. Nasim couldn't understand why no one of his kind had taken her as their Chosen, for she was certainly lovely enough. Perhaps her spirit was so fierce that the djinn who'd decided to save a human for their eternal partner had determined it would be safer to claim someone a bit more biddable.

Whatever the reason, she certainly appeared to be on her own. The rumor was that she had been with a group of survivors on the run not too far from here, but that the rest of them had been caught and killed. Whether that was true or not made no real difference to him. It only mattered that she had given him a purpose, something to occupy his time. Sooner or later this game would have to end, he supposed, but in the meantime, he might as well enjoy himself.

However, it seemed he would have to change his tactics. With an impatient gesture, he blinked himself back to the loft he had taken for his use while hunting his quarry. Downtown Los Angeles was a no man's land in terms of the djinn population; no one lived here permanently, for all the djinn who'd been given lands in Southern California were farther inland, in less developed areas. There was a community of djinn and their Chosen not too far away in a place called Bel-Air, but again, they had no reason to come to L.A.'s dead city center.

The loft was certainly not the largest or the most luxurious in the area, but it was comfortable, and offered breathtaking views of the city. There was also a rooftop deck and swimming pool. Although he had yet to bother with the pool, he had to admit that it was quite pleasant to sit up on the deck and drink wine and watch the city, eyes always scanning the streets below for any sign of movement. Several times he'd spied the woman's bright blue car from this vantage point, but it had never been close enough that he'd been able to catch up with her before she disappeared again. His inborn talent for blinking himself from place to place was of no real use here, for she was wily enough that he hadn't yet been able to antici-pate her movements and place himself where he expected her to be. Clearly, she knew the streets and alleys of the downtown area far better than he.

Still wearing a frown, Nasim snapped his fingers and called a glass of white wine to himself. It appeared, a cool glass of Viognier, perfect for quenching his thirst after yet another fruitless pursuit on a warm day.

The thought that the woman was so adept at evading capture annoyed him. What irritated him even more was that he, a djinn, should have easily been able to catch her. Did he not command the power of the air? Could he not fly faster than the swiftest bird?

Well, it did not seem to matter much, because her car was much, much faster.

Her car was so much faster....

Of course. Nasim took a large swallow of wine and wanted to shake his head at himself. Why on earth had he not thought of it before this? The solution was really so simple, it should have occurred to him the very first time he saw that sleek, sky-hued vehicle disappear around a corner and leave him in the proverbial dust.

If he wanted the situation to change, then he must change it. And that meant forgetting what he knew, and learning something he did not. He smiled as he thought of the surprise that would touch her face, the shock as she realized he had brought the fight to her.

As he drank his wine, he wondered how long it would take him to learn to drive a car....

TWO

ONE OF THE ITEMS BAILEY HAD TAKEN during her foraging expeditions was a small wall calendar, the kind of thing auto parts manufacturers used to give out for free. Thank God that this one only had innocuous images of iconic Los Angeles locations, rather than girls in bikinis, since she'd seen enough of those hanging on the walls of the garages where she'd worked to last her a lifetime. But she would have taken the calendar even if it had included gratuitous T&A, because she wanted to make sure she kept an accurate record of the passage of time. It was now early May, and she'd left the Caltech group only a few days into October.

By any sort of estimation, that was a hell of a long time to be alone, she supposed, but Bailey had a feeling her solitude was part of what had saved her. At any rate, it wasn't the date itself that disturbed her now, but the realization that the new djinn had come on the scene ten days ago, and it had been four days since she'd last seen him. Had he, too, given up?

Who knew djinn could be this lazy? she thought as she drank the last of the water from her bottle and then carefully stowed the trash in the trunk of the Porsche. At first it had seemed almost criminal to use her beloved 911 for that purpose, but she made sure to bag everything before she disposed of it elsewhere. There were plenty of dumpsters around downtown, and she figured it was smarter not to leave trash behind in the places where she crashed. At least that way the djinn couldn't track her simply by the garbage she created.

Well, if this latest djinn had bailed, for whatever reason, then she could be pretty sure that another one would show up soon enough to take his place. Too bad, because he was damn cute.

Not that it mattered one way or another, of course, but it was always nice to have something pretty to look at in her rearview mirror.

Once the place where she'd slept was tidied up, she went ahead and got in the Porsche and started it. The fuel gauge read that the tank was three-quarters empty. She carried a gas can in the trunk, but that was for dire emergencies.

Time to go out siphoning. It was a lot easier than going to a gas station and setting the pumps to manual. Bailey knew how to do that, but there weren't a lot of gas stations in the downtown area, and she felt hinky about getting too far from any of her hidey holes. Better to just grab what she needed from one of downtown's abandoned vehicles. God only knew that there seemed to be an unending supply of those. In her bug-out bag, she carried a small notebook to keep track of the cars she'd already drained; leaving any kind of physical mark on those cars might have given the djinn a clue as to her whereabouts. Having her own private diary seemed safer. At the back of her mind lurked the constant worry about what she'd do when the gas contained in those abandoned cars finally began to go bad, but she told herself she had far bigger problems to deal with right now. After all, while she of course preferred to drive, she knew she could always get away from Los Angeles on foot if need be.

She eased the car up the ramp of the parking garage and paused for a second to look around and get her bearings. As always, the streets were empty. Today, though, the morning felt dreary and almost creepy, thanks to a thick fog that had moved in overnight. Typical for this time of year —"May gray" often gave way to "June gloom," thanks to the marine layer that tended to lurk off

Southern California's coast—but she hated it all the same. When the weather was like this, it always aroused thoughts of zombie apocalypses and hordes of undead crowding the streets, although intellectually Bailey knew this wasn't *that* kind of end of the world.

The fog was just thick enough that she couldn't see farther than a few blocks. It wisped around the high-rises, transformed the sun to a pale, ineffectual disk. As much as she would have liked to turn on her low-beams, she knew that wasn't a very good idea. No, she'd just have to creep along until she got to an area that she hadn't drained dry yet.

Luckily, she didn't have to drive more than a few blocks. Spotting a big Mercedes S-Class parked in front of the U.S. Bank Tower, Bailey came to a stop and got out of the Porsche, then hurried back to the trunk to get out the hose she used for siphoning gas, along with the gas can that traveled everywhere with her. While the 911 could run on lower-octane fuel, it was always better to get the premium stuff if she could, which was why she'd made the Mercedes her target.

The S-Class wasn't locked. She saw why soon enough—a neat pile of gray dust on the driver's seat, presumably the car's former owner. Ignoring the dust, she went back and popped open the little door in the right rear of the vehicle, then removed the gas cap.

It was hard to find something that tasted fouler than gasoline, but she was so used to siphoning the stuff that by this point, she hardly noticed. The liquid began to pour into the gas can, pattering against the plastic. On a dim, foggy morning like this, every sound seemed amplified, and she winced at the noise she was making. Then again, who was around to hear? Even her latest pursuer seemed to have decamped, tired of pursuing her, just like every other djinn who'd crossed her path.

But then a low, growling noise reached her ears, one that seemed to grow louder with every passing second. Bailey glanced around but saw nothing, only wisps of fog curling their way around the corners of the buildings, shrouding the tops of the high-rises in gloom.

A pair of headlights raked through the fog. She startled, so shocked by the unexpected sight that she dropped the siphon hose to the ground. Gas began to spill onto the pavement, but she realized that the leaking fuel was the least of her worries as out of the fog came a flash of bright red, a car so preposterously sleek that it took a moment for her shocked brain to register what it was.

A fucking Ferrari?!

Instinct kicked in, and she ran to the Porsche and jumped inside, foot hitting the accelerator even as she slammed the door shut, the abandoned fuel can and siphon hose still lying on the street. She didn't stop to think that possibly the Ferrari's driver could be another survivor. Somehow she knew it couldn't be, not when she hadn't seen another human being for more than six months.

The headlights were in her rearview mirror, coming closer. Bailey fought with the seatbelt as she drove, at last hearing it click into place as she careened around the corner at Third and Los Angeles Street, heading north and east. The fog had dampened the road surface just enough that it was faintly slick, and she could feel the rear tires begin to slip. Luckily, the traction control caught, but her fingers tightened on the steering wheel nonetheless. At these speeds, it didn't take much to end up in a world of hurt if you weren't careful.

Just drive, she told herself, forcing her eyes away from the rearview. Driving by mirror was an easy way to screw up. She needed to keep her focus forward, on the road ahead. Obsessing over what her pursuer was doing would only slow her down.

Still, she couldn't help but wonder where the hell he'd gotten a Ferrari. If her faceless pursuer was even the "he" she was thinking of. For all she knew, that really was another survivor coming after her, and she was going to feel like a complete idiot once the truth came out.

Her instincts were telling her otherwise, however.

Screaming onto Grand now, taking a loop around the music center complex that included the Ahmanson and the Dorothy Chandler Pavilion and the Mark Taper Forum. Bailey knew those venues only as names, since she'd never had the cash or the inclination to attend the kinds of performances that used to be held there. The fog seemed thinner in this part of town, and she risked a quick look back at the Ferrari, now only a few yards away from her rear bumper. It was close enough that she could see through the windshield, could see the sharp, handsome features of the djinn who'd been her pursuer up until a few days ago.

Shit.

Since when could djinn *drive?*

Since now, apparently. Bailey wanted to believe that her eyes were deceiving her, but she'd always had 20/20 vision, so she knew what she'd seen was real. That was a djinn behind the wheel of the red Ferrari, and the only thing left to do was pray like hell that her driving skills were better than his.

As she turned down Hope Street, she saw a

carve-out to her left, one that had probably once been used for valet parking at the Music Center. It was unoccupied now, only a few abandoned cars left to mark its former purpose. However, past it was a wide open space, one that still held a few kiosks and concrete picnic tables, the umbrellas overhead now faded and torn after spending months and months out in the wind and weather. Bailey didn't care about the umbrellas, though. What she cared about was the obvious escape route that open expanse offered her. She could cut across there and drop back down to Grand, lose herself in the streets she knew so well. The djinn pursuing her would never expect that kind of crazy maneuver.

Without stopping to think, she took her foot off the gas, manually downshifted into third, then made a sharp left, pushing the Porsche over the curbs that separated the valet area from Hope Street. The car bounced but kept going, its traction control making sure that she experienced only the tiniest bit of oversteer before the 911 righted itself and kept going.

From behind her, she heard a squeal of brakes as the Ferrari turned to follow. Damn it. Another quick glance in the rearview, one that told her the djinn had no compunction about pushing a quarter million dollars' worth of Italian engineering over those same curbs. True, she'd abused her Porsche, but at least she knew how to fix it if something broke.

No time to worry about that now. She careened across what used to be the Music Center's famous in-ground fountain, her teeth gritted against the further jouncing caused by the uneven surface, fingers clenched on the steering wheel. Grand Avenue was coming up fast.

Only—

Shit. *Shit.*

Stairs.

Steep, steep stairs, heading down from the Music Center's level to Grand Avenue below. She'd forgotten about the complex's underground parking, the way it was carved into the hillside.

Foot off the gas, hitting the brakes, downshifting frantically into second gear. The Porsche slowed, but not enough. The tires hit the top step, slipped, the traction control finding nothing to latch onto. Tilting now, rear end fishtailing on the damp cement. Bailey bit her lip, bit it so hard she could taste the metallic tang of her own blood. A sickening sensation hit her stomach as the Porsche began to roll, crunching its way down the steps.

After it crashed into one of the retaining walls to either side of the staircase, the front end crumpling like a giant's fist had just smashed into the metal, darkness descended and took her far away.

Nasim saw the bright blue car hit the stairs, tires screeching. In horror, he watched it begin to flip, then roll its way down the steep staircase that led to the street on the south side of the Music Center complex. He might have suffered the same fate—he'd taught himself to drive but couldn't consider himself an expert—if it weren't that he used his djinn powers to gather the air and use it as a cushion to slow down the vehicle he drove, helping the brakes do their job. Because of this, the car stopped a few inches from the steps that had proved to be the young woman's downfall.

Without hesitating, he blinked himself out of the Ferrari and down to street level, where the Porsche had landed on its side. The sleek metal was now horribly scored and crumpled, but the center of the vehicle seemed more or less intact.

Thank God.

He hurried over to the car, grasped the driver-side door, and wrenched it open. The young woman was still in her seat, held in place by the safety belt she wore. Her eyes were shut, and blood obscured half her face.

But he could tell she still breathed.

At once his fingers were on the seatbelt, unfastening it so he could lift her out of the wreck of the Porsche. Her body was so limp that he feared the worst, but after he'd laid her down on the asphalt and put a shaking hand on her throat to feel her pulse, he could tell she was still alive. How badly injured, he didn't know for sure. She could have broken bones, internal bleeding…in which case, there was not very much he could do for her. His people, blessed with endless health and eternal youth, had very little need of healers.

Still, he would have to try.

He gathered her in his arms. She did not move, made no protest, which told him she must be lost in deep unconsciousness. And while he understood why she had fled, he could not help but feel a flash of irrational anger at her for doing this to herself. If she had not tried so hard to run away….

No, that was being unfair. She had no reason to believe she would not have suffered the same fate as all her people, if he had managed to catch up with her.

A blink, and they were in his loft. Nasim carried her over to the bedroom and pulled aside the bedclothes, then laid her gently down. He did not wish to wound her further by struggling to remove the leather jacket she wore, or her heavy boots, and so he snapped his fingers and whisked those troublesome items away to the closet. Another snap, and a bowl of warm water and a soft cloth appeared.

He bent and carefully wiped the blood from her face. There was a gash on her forehead, probably caused by flying glass from the Porsche's windshield. It could have been much worse, although the wound bled freely enough, as such things often did. He dabbed at it until the flow of blood slowed and then seemed to stop. Good. That was better.

Now that her jacket was gone, he could see that the flesh around her collarbone was already beginning to turn rather alarming shades of purple and blue. Very carefully, he laid his fingers against the bone beneath the skin, could feel the broken edges grind under his fingertips.

No wonder she had fainted. It had probably been a defense against the pain.

Nasim was glad that she was safely unconscious, because he doubted she would have liked what he had to do next. Just as he had whisked away her jacket and boots, he did the same with her blood-soaked T-shirt and jeans so he might see what other injuries she had suffered.

However, as he ran his hands over her arms and then her legs and sternum, he could find no other signs of anything broken. Bumps and bruises, of course, but those would heal quickly enough. It was the broken collarbone that caused him the most concern.

It had fractured on the left side, which meant

he should keep her left arm immobile. More than once in his journeys around the city, he'd noted the hospital on the outskirts of downtown. It required only a few seconds to blink himself there, a few more to read the directory and locate the orthopedic ward. A bit of rummaging in the supply room provided the sling he sought. To be safe, he took several, along with a couple of hospital gowns, then returned to his loft.

The woman was still unconscious. Even so, he was careful when approaching the bed. He guessed she would not be happy with him for removing her clothes, and so he put one of the gowns on her, then eased her left arm into the sling. As he worked, she made a few whimpering sounds, but those must have been born of reflex and nothing else, since she showed no sign of waking.

Then he was done, her left arm safely immobilized, her slender body now modestly covered once more. Nasim tried not to think too much about how beautiful that body was, even bruised and battered from the accident. Her legs were long, her waist slender, her breasts—what he could see of them in the plain white bra she wore —rounded and full.

And her face….

Nasim had been in Florence during the Renaissance, had seen the magnificent art created there. If Botticelli had caught even a glimpse of this lovely young woman, he would surely have wished to paint her.

But there were few mortals left to paint now, and Nasim knew he did not possess that particular skill. He could only be relieved that the young woman had survived the crash. Her recovery would be slow, he assumed, but since she otherwise seemed healthy enough, he thought she should be fine, given enough time.

However, he doubted she would be pleased to find herself here when she awoke.

THREE

EVERY MUSCLE IN HER BODY HURT. HER HEAD pounded, and there was an especially alarming dull ache in her collarbone, one that told her she'd been injured, and probably pretty badly.

Far more alarming than that, however, was the man who sat at her bedside and peered down at her with far more concern in his eyes than she'd expected.

Blue. They were a pure, piercing blue, just like she'd thought they would be.

"Wha—?" The word came out in a croak, and she immediately started coughing.

"Here," he said, holding out a glass of water. "Can you drink?"

Could she? Probably. He sat on her right side, on her uninjured side.

No, scratch that. Her *less* injured side. Her

shoulder throbbed, and she could see bruises and scrapes on her arm as she lifted it to take the water from him. Still, she was able to move, even though she had to grit her teeth against the pain. God, she would have killed for some Percocet right then.

However, since no pills appeared to be forthcoming, she drank the water and tried not to wince. Although he must have known the extent of her injuries—she was under no illusions as to who had put her in this hospital gown, or slipped her arm into its sling—Bailey still didn't want him to know how much everything hurt. Better to concentrate on what the hell she was doing here. This had to be his place, or at least the place he'd been using as a home base while he tried to hunt her down. It looked expensive, in a kind of industrial way. A loft, probably, one of those little downtown L.A. jobs that would set you back a cool million or so for something less than fifteen hundred square feet.

Not that a djinn had to worry about the price of real estate. It wasn't as though the original owner of this place needed it anymore.

It was easier to think about that, or about how the djinn seemed to speak perfect English, than to think about how badly she'd screwed up…or how scared she was.

Staring at him, she asked, "Why aren't I dead?"

He said, "The seatbelt kept you from being ejected from the vehicle. And I assume it had some sort of infrastructure that prevented the passenger compartment from being crushed, although I don't know much about vehicle safety engineering."

Which was actually a fairly accurate assessment as to why she wasn't a damp spot in the middle of Grand Avenue. However, that wasn't the true answer.

Still holding his gaze, she said, "You know that's not what I asked."

Not even a blink. This close, she could see the thick brown lashes that fringed his blue eyes, the strong lines of his chin, the sharply sculpted nose and fine cheekbones. Almost model-pretty, but there was an edge to him that she doubted most male models had ever possessed. And then there was that killer body, barely concealed by the open sleeveless robe he wore—one that was now smudged with blood.

Her blood.

With the faintest lift of one eyebrow, he said, "You mean, why haven't I killed you?"

She pressed her lips together and nodded.

"I didn't want to."

"Why not?" Bailey took another sip of water

and asked, her tone deliberately hard, "Isn't that what you djinn do?"

"So, you know what I am."

"Yes." At the beginning, she hadn't wanted to believe it. She'd wanted to think that the crazy man on the radio, the one from the Los Alamos labs whom the Caltech group had been briefly in contact with, had been babbling, driven insane by all the death around him. It hadn't been too hard to believe that that particular mad scientist had made up his whacked-out theory about other-worldly creatures creating the disease that destroyed the world.

Unlike some of the others, Bailey hadn't yet seen a djinn murder anyone. When the world fell apart, people dropping like flies everywhere and turning to dust, she'd taken a car from the shop where she'd been working in El Monte and headed north, having the vague idea that maybe hiding out in the high desert around Lancaster or Palmdale would be safe. It was then that Tyrell Johnson flagged her down as she drove along Lake Avenue, dodging abandoned cars. He'd told her that it wasn't safe to drive, that she'd be caught if she wasn't careful.

Not too long after that, she first heard about the djinn from the man on the radio. Miles Odekirk. Of course, the real problem was that even though what he was saying sounded crazy, *he* didn't sound particularly crazy, was too calm, if anything. And Bailey hadn't figured out what to do about that.

Anyway, she knew what the djinn were, how they had made sure to kill every human being who hadn't been felled by the Heat.

"Ah," the djinn said after a long pause, apparently deciding how he should approach this. "I am not a reaver like those you've seen at work since the Dying. I have no wish to kill you."

"Then why were you chasing me?"

"Because…." The word trailed off as he seemed to gather his thoughts. "Because I had heard about you, about an elusive woman in downtown Los Angeles whom no one seemed able to capture. I thought I would come here and try for myself."

He made it sound as though she was some rare white tiger he was hunting down. Actually, that might be exactly how he saw her. Worthy prey, something to occupy his time. Was she supposed to be flattered by his appraisal of her? She didn't know. Her brain hurt, and she didn't want to think about that possibility.

Another question crept into her brain, however. What was it djinn did when they weren't killing humans?

"Well, you succeeded," she said. "You've caught me. Now what?"

"I'm not sure," he replied. "That last chase, in the cars. It was quite…exhilarating."

That wasn't the word she would have used for it. More like terrifying. Then again, she'd been sure he would murder her the second he caught up with her, but that didn't seem to be his plan…unless he was trying to make her think he was harmless so that the shock from him attacking her later would be that much more intense.

It sounded like the kind of sick shit that a djinn might get off on.

"Glad you had fun," she remarked, shifting slightly, teeth clenched. She'd been in a few minor fender-benders, but she'd never crashed a car before this. Now she knew why. It *sucked*.

"You're in pain," he said, obviously catching how she'd winced, even though she'd done her best to conceal how much the slightest movement sent fresh waves of agony moving through her battered frame.

"No shit, Sherlock," she replied. Right then, she really didn't care if she offended him. After all, if he killed her, she wouldn't hurt anymore.

Rather than looking annoyed, he appeared more worried by her current condition than anything else. "What can I do for you?"

"Drugs," Bailey said promptly. "You had to have gotten this sling and this hospital gown from somewhere, so you can go back for some drugs. I need painkillers. Percocet, or some oxy."

"'Oxy'?" he repeated, expression confused.

"Ox-y-contin," she said slowly. "A shot of Demerol would be nice, but I can live without that. And some Betadine or some kind of topical antiseptic for all these cuts and scrapes."

The djinn nodded, brow furrowed as though he was carefully committing all her requests to memory. "I know where to get them. You will not try to escape while I'm gone?"

She gave him a mocking smile. "I've got a broken collarbone, bumps and bruises up the yin-yang, and I'm in a hospital gown with my ass hanging out. Exactly where do you think I would go?"

The serious, intent expression he wore didn't change. "I see your point." He got up from the chair where he'd been sitting, then added, "I won't be long."

And after that, he just…vanished. Poof—right into thin air. Bailey had seen djinn pop in and out of existence during all those times they'd been chasing her, but it was even more disconcerting to have it happen right in front of your face. She thought she even heard a faint *pop!*, as though air had rushed in to fill the void he'd left behind. But she couldn't be sure about that. Everything hurt so much, she couldn't be sure of anything right then.

Except that somehow, miraculously, she was still alive.

———————

Nasim returned to the hospital and went in search of the items the young woman had requested. There was a pharmacy on the ground floor, and that seemed to be the most logical place to look for the drugs Bailey had requested. Percocet, and the one with the even stranger name.

Oxycontin.

He thought he didn't much like the sound of that one, but he supposed much depended on what he found. The pharmacy had clearly been ransacked as the Heat gripped the city, and many of the shelves were empty or in complete disarray. However, he dutifully hunted through the mess and at last found a bottle of the Percocet she'd requested.

The first aid supplies were in better shape, luckily. He found a big bottle marked "Betadine" and took that, along with gauze pads and adhesive tape and anything else that looked as though it might be useful. There were plastic bags stashed behind the counter, and he pulled one out and filled it with his loot, then blinked back to the loft.

Despite her protestations to the contrary,

he'd halfway expected the young woman to be gone. However, as he entered the bedroom, he saw that she was still there, eyes shut, fingers clutched in the sheets as though she held on to them in an attempt to counteract the pain she must be experiencing, since she had nothing else.

"I'm back," he said softly.

At once her eyes opened. Big and blue, like the sky. Despite her obvious pain, a little color had returned to her cheeks, and he assumed that must be a good sign. "Did you find the stuff I asked for?"

"Yes." He came over to her bedside and set the bag down on the table there, then got out the bottle of Percocet and tapped one of the tablets into his palm. "Here."

She took it from him and dry-swallowed it, then lay back against the pillows, eyes half shut.

"Better?"

Her head turned slightly. One corner of her mouth quirked. "It doesn't work quite that fast."

"Oh." Nasim supposed he should have realized that, but his experience with human medications was far from extensive. Even though she'd already taken the pill, he went ahead and held out her half-drunk glass of water. "You should have some of this."

Without replying, she took the glass and

drank most of its contents, then gave it back to him.

He put it on the bedside table. "Let me clean your wounds. You don't want them to become infected."

"In a minute." Eyes shut, she breathed in and out. "It's probably better to let the drug take effect before we start on that."

Perhaps she was right. The broken collarbone was her most serious injury, but she had bruises and lacerations everywhere. Giving the Percocet time to dull the pain would make the ordeal a bit less onerous.

"If you wish," he said. "What is your name?"

"Does it matter?"

"Yes."

One blue eye cracked open and slanted him a sideways glance. "Why?"

"Because if I am going to take care of you, then I feel I should know your name."

A faint sigh escaped her lips. Nasim could tell that she did not much care to be reminded of her current injured, helpless state. But then she said, "Bailey. Bailey O'Keefe."

It was not the most euphonious of names, but in a way, it suited her. "And I am Nasim al-Jibril."

Her mouth twitched slightly. "You sound like a rapper."

He frowned at her, not sure what she meant.

Possibly the drug she had taken had already begun to scramble her brain a bit. Deciding to put the matter aside, he asked, "How do you feel?"

"Better…." The word trailed off, and her eyes closed. However, she wasn't asleep, because she said, "Go ahead, doctor. Right now, I'm feeling no pain…or maybe I'm feeling it, but I just don't care. Either way, you're good to go."

Nasim assumed that was her way of saying the Percocet had begun to take hold. He went ahead and got the bottle of Betadine out of the bag he'd taken from the hospital, then poured some on one of the gauze pads and went to work on the worst of her wounds, the cut on her scalp. She winced slightly as the antiseptic liquid touched her skin, but she didn't try to pull away, only kept her eyes shut as he worked.

Her leather jacket had protected her arms from cuts and lacerations, but she had scrapes on the knuckles of both hands, and several on her neck as well. Very carefully, he pushed her long blonde braid out of the way so he could dab at the cuts on her throat. He hoped that they would heal without leaving a scar; her skin was smooth and pale, with a rose-petal texture that made him want to linger there.

Or possibly bend down and touch his lips to her soft flesh.

Just the mere thought was enough to make his

body begin to respond, and he resolutely pushed it away. This woman was wounded…and human, both very good reasons not to touch her, except as needed to help her recover from her injuries. Many years ago, when he could consider himself still young, he had taken a mortal woman as his lover, but that had not gone well. She had not known him for what he was, and thought that he would become her husband. Of course such an outcome was impossible, and he'd been forced to leave. Even now, the memory was not one he cared to revisit, although he told himself he should, if for no other reason than to remind himself that human women should be off limits. He had decided that he did not want to take a Chosen, although he had nothing against those who had determined it was their fate to save at least one human. His destiny had lain along a different path.

Although he was damned if he knew what it was.

The remainder of Bailey's injuries were bumps and bruises, and there was little he could do about those, except allow time to heal them, as it did most wounds. Her clothing had protected her from far worse injuries, for he'd seen the glass scattered everywhere, had known it would have cut into her arms and legs if she hadn't been wearing that leather jacket, those thick jeans and boots.

"All done," he said as he put the Betadine back down. "Do you feel better?"

She smiled, a slow, lazy smile that at once sent heat stirring in his loins, even though he knew that smile probably had very little to do with his presence. "I feel great. I should probably be worried about being alone here with a djinn, but right now I just don't care."

"You have nothing to worry about, Bailey," he said, doing his best to make his tone as soothing as possible. "Perhaps you should try to sleep for a while. If you're hungry when you wake up, I'll see about getting you some food."

"Yes, doctor," she replied demurely, then giggled a little. Her right hand went to her mouth, as though she thought she should silence herself. "Don't do drugs, kids."

And then she giggled again.

Although Nasim couldn't say he knew her very well—or at all, really—he guessed this behavior was somewhat out of character for her. It seemed she was right about the deleterious effects of taking drugs.

But now that she had them in her system, probably best to let her sleep...and hope she might be more herself when she awoke.

Bailey opened her eyes. The pain had receded to a dull throb. She knew it was there, but the Percocet was allowing her to mostly ignore it. Even so, she took a quick inventory—scrapes on her knuckles, a sting along the edge of her scalp to remind her of the gash she'd suffered there, bruised elbows and knees. The worst of it was that damn collarbone, but she supposed she was lucky to have gotten off that lightly. The djinn—Nasim, she reminded herself—had pulled her from the wreckage of the Porsche, but she supposed she could have walked away on her own, once she'd regained consciousness.

For a moment she lay there, eyes fixed on the high ceiling, which seemed to be made of painted boards. A few exposed pipes were visible. Not a lot, just enough to remind you that this had once been an industrial building, even if now it had been turned into a bunch of very expensive lofts. It didn't seem like a very djinn-ish place, but Bailey had to admit she didn't know much about the otherworldly creatures who'd apparently decided to take over now that humankind was mostly out of the way.

What she really couldn't figure out was why Nasim hadn't killed her. He'd made it sound as if the thrill of chasing her was his only goal, but that didn't seem quite right. Even if it might have been at one point, now she sure as hell wasn't the worthy adversary he sought, not after crashing her car like that. What was the point in keeping her around if she couldn't even drive? Maybe that thought should have made her anxious, but right then she was floating on a Percocet high, and nothing seemed to trouble her very much.

Soft footsteps made her glance toward the doorway, which wasn't even a true doorway, but rather an opening in some sliding panels made of wood and frosted glass to give the impression of a wall. Nasim stood just outside, his expression unreadable. To her surprise, he'd changed out of what she'd assumed must be his djinn clothing, and into a black long-sleeved T-shirt and some jeans. Once again she was hit by the impression that he could have been some guy she'd met at a street race, and with her brain as fogged by the Percocet as it now was, she had a hard time reminding herself that he wasn't really a man at all.

"You're awake," he said. "I went to the central library and fetched a book on first aid. It said I should put some ice on the fracture to bring down the swelling."

That sounded common-sense enough, although right then Bailey was feeling warm and snuggly and sort of drifting. The idea of putting a freezing cold ice pack on her collarbone didn't seem all that appealing. Still, she knew she needed to do whatever she could to heal up, although she wasn't looking forward to the process. Even for someone in their twenties and in perfect health, that kind of healing would take weeks. Was Nasim really planning to keep her here and play nurse-maid for that long?

"Okay," she said, since it didn't make much sense to turn down his offer.

"I'll go get the ice, then."

He disappeared, but in the normal way, walking toward what she presumed must be the loft's kitchen, although she couldn't see much from where she lay. Gingerly, she pushed herself up to a sitting position, using her uninjured right arm for leverage. Right across from her was more of that frosted glass, this time installed in panels that concealed a closet that stretched from wall to wall, one that was actually installed on the oppo-site side of the hallway. A bunch of clothes still hung in that closet, and none of it looked like djinn stuff. Nasim must have left the previous owner's clothing there for some reason.

A moment later, he returned, holding an actual ice pack and not just a baggie filled with ice cubes. Bailey was somewhat relieved by that, since past injuries had told her that a single ice pack was a lot easier to manage. Nasim came over to her, then pushed her braid out of the way and slipped the cold pack under the strap of the sling she wore.

It was strange to have him so close, to look down and see his deft, sun-browned fingers so close to her skin, to breathe in the warm, enticing scent that drifted from his longish hair. As much as she wanted to shrink away, she forced herself to sit still and stare off into the distance as he worked.

When he was done, he straightened up and took a step away from the bed. "Better?"

Actually, it wasn't, because now that she had the ice pack touching her skin, it seemed to reawaken all the nerve endings in the swollen flesh around the fracture. However, she thought it would sound pretty rude to point that out, so she only replied, "It'll definitely bring the swelling down, and that's good, because you don't want it pushing the fractured bone out of place. Otherwise, it might not knit together right."

"You sound as if you know something about it."

She wanted to shrug, but decided against it, since it would probably hurt too much. "I fell off my bike and broke my arm when I was twelve. Really pissed off the fosters."

"'The Fosters'?" he repeated. "Is that the name of the people who raised you?"

Despite the situation, she couldn't help but

chuckle at his obvious confusion. "No, they were my foster parents. Do you know what that means?"

"You were raised by people who weren't your birth family?"

That was a polite way of putting it. She'd been unceremoniously dumped at a fire station in Pasadena, umbilical cord still attached, with only a block-printed note that said, *Her name is Bailey.* Oh, she'd been fostered fairly quickly, because people always wanted pretty little blonde, blue-eyed babies, and the family who'd taken her in began adoption proceedings almost at once. Unfortunately, the adoption was never finalized, because when she was a little past a year old, Madeline, her first foster mother, found herself pregnant after all, and they couldn't afford two kids. That was when Bailey went back into the system and didn't come out again until she was eighteen and sent out on her own with just the clothes she owned and a thousand bucks to get started in her new life.

Actually, after dealing with all that, surviving the end of the world didn't seem so tough.

"No," she said, her tone deliberately hard. "I don't know who my parents were. Ward of the state and all that crap."

Nasim only nodded, which could have meant that he'd gotten her meaning, or that he was puzzled by the whole thing but didn't want to seem ignorant. Either way, it really didn't matter all that much. His next question surprised her, though. "Why would your foster parents be angry with you for breaking your arm? I would think they'd be worried you were injured."

"Because broken arms cost money, even when the state reimburses you," Bailey replied. "Not to mention lost time at work because of having to haul some kid to the emergency room, and then the doctor later to get the cast taken off."

"They weren't concerned for your well-being?"

There was a joke. She swallowed, pushing away memories that she'd spent years working to keep safely buried. "No," she said carelessly, "they just wanted to make sure they kept getting those checks for my room and board every month."

Once again, Nasim appeared confused. To her relief, however, he seemed content to let the matter go, because he asked next, "Could you eat something?"

The mere mention of food made Bailey's stomach rumble. She'd had a protein bar for breakfast, but that had been hours ago, and now the Percocet felt like acid in her empty belly. "I could," she said, although she tried not to sound too enthusiastic. "It depends on what, I guess."

This time he smiled. He had very white teeth, perfect as though he had spent years in braces, although she guessed he'd come by that flashing smile naturally. "Whatever you would like. Food is something we can easily manage."

Like blinking in and out of existence as if it was nothing. Faced with a world of possibilities, Bailey wasn't sure what she wanted. It had been so long since she'd had anything decent to eat, something warm that actually filled her stomach, rather than providing just enough fuel so she wouldn't starve outright.

"A grilled cheese sandwich and tomato soup," she said, then added, "please."

If Nasim noticed how tacked-on that "please" had been, he didn't show any sign of it. "Not a problem."

And then, without any ceremony, there it was, sitting on a tray that suddenly appeared on her lap —a grilled cheese, perfectly golden and with enough of its contents oozing out between the two slices of bread that she could see it had several different kinds of cheese inside, and a small bowl of tomato soup with an island of shredded cheese floating in the center.

Oh, my God.

Maybe if the Percocet hadn't been dulling the edges of her synapses, she might have been more curious as to how he'd been able to make a complete meal appear out of thin air like that. However, right then she was too hungry to care.

She picked up one half of the sandwich and bit into it.

Heaven. Yes, that was heaven right there, in jack and cheddar cheese and toasted sourdough, all melded into perfect melted harmony. She took another bite, and another, and only paused when she realized Nasim was watching her with what looked like a mixture of amusement and curiosity, one eyebrow tilted slightly upward.

"Good?"

"Yes," she said. "It's really good. Thanks. Sorry I went into wolf mode there. It's just been a long time since I had anything decent to eat."

The amusement faded from his expression, replaced by something that looked almost like pity. She didn't like that. She didn't want to be pitied. Her existence hadn't been exactly luxurious lately, but she'd gotten by. Then he said those two words she hated to hear.

"I'm sorry."

"Don't be." Bailey set down her grilled cheese and reached for the spoon that rested on the tray. As she dipped it into the tomato soup, she added, "It's not your fault." Or actually…. "Well, I guess it kind of is, isn't it? Anyway, thanks for the food."

"You're welcome." His tone was stiff, and she got the impression she'd offended him with that last comment. Luckily, the Percocet kept her from caring very much. "I'll come back for the tray later." Then he turned and left the room.

Yes, she'd definitely offended him. Well, either he'd get over it or he wouldn't. For the moment, she just wanted to eat and enjoy the sensation of actually being full. She was safe, wasn't she? If Nasim really wanted to hurt her, she doubted he'd be giving her painkillers and ice packs and trays of hot food.

At least, that was what she told herself as she continued to eat. She really didn't want to contemplate the alternative.

FOUR

Nasim didn't know why Bailey's words had irritated him so much. After all, on the surface, they'd been true enough. If it weren't for the djinn and the havoc they'd wreaked on this world, she wouldn't have been forced to spend more than half a year on the run, grabbing what food she could, never having enough.

Then again, judging by those few details she'd just told him about her childhood, it didn't sound as though she'd ever had much.

Despite his irritation, pity moved through him. He did not pretend to know everything about the intricacies of human civilization, but it sounded as though Bailey had been one of those forgotten children who never had a true home or a family who cared for her. No wonder she was so prickly, even with the potent drug she'd taken doing its best to file down some of her sharper edges. His own distant childhood had been happy enough, with parents who remained together long after he reached adulthood in his second decade, and so he could not quite understand all that Bailey had suffered during her own youth. Whatever it had been, it was enough to make her strong, or she would never have been able to survive in this greatly altered world for so long.

He wondered where she'd learned to drive. Her skills were far above those of a normal commuter, despite the way she'd crashed her vehicle while trying to escape him. She'd been desperate, frightened, or the accident would have never happened.

Enough time had passed that he thought he had better go and take her meal tray away. Their last exchange had been a bit sharp, but nothing that couldn't be smoothed over. He knew he needed to get along with her, for her convalescence would take a while, even though she was young and otherwise seemed healthy enough.

When he came to the entrance of the loft's only bedroom, he saw that she was asleep again, tray still covering her lap. In fact, the spoon he had provided was still in her right hand, drooping against the covers.

Something taut and controlled about her expression disappeared in sleep. She looked younger and softer, even though he knew she must be quite young as humans counted such things. Still, he had the impression that she'd already seen far too much in her short life.

Moving carefully, he went to her bedside and took the spoon from her limp fingers. She stirred, but not enough to wake all the way. Nasim set the spoon on the tray and lifted it from her lap, then began to head toward the doorway. Her voice stopped him before he got to the hall.

"Sorry."

Startled, he turned around to see her watching him, blue eyes blurry with sleep but still aware. "Sorry for what?"

"I was being a bitch. You didn't deserve it."

"I think you're being too hard on yourself. You are in pain."

"And on drugs." She smiled slightly, but it was an inward-turned, deprecating smile, not one especially meant for him. "I guess I just don't understand."

"Understand what?"

"Why you're taking care of me."

Bailey might not have understood, but Nasim thought he did. Or at least, he guessed she wasn't used to anyone fussing over her, since it seemed clear enough that her foster parents had done no such thing. "It was because of me that you crashed your car. The least I can do is make sure you recover from your injuries."

"Oh." She appeared to ponder those words for a moment, her smile gone, mouth drooping. "It was a good car. It didn't deserve to end up like that."

Her sadness was so palpable, Nasim had to fight the urge to set down the tray he carried and go over and take her in his arms to comfort her. However, he thought she wouldn't much appreciate such a gesture, even if he could accomplish that kind of maneuver without jostling her wounded shoulder.

"It is unfortunate," he said carefully, even as an idea occurred to him. Perhaps it would take a while for her fractured collarbone to heal, but there was one thing he knew he could fix. "But the important thing is that you survived, and that you will heal. It was just a car."

"I guess so," she replied, her tone dubious.

"Rest now," Nasim told her. "That is what you need more than anything else."

She nodded, but her expression was still wistful. However, she closed her eyes and shifted slightly on the pillows, obviously attempting to find a position that wouldn't put pressure on her broken bone.

Nasim took that as his signal to leave. He went down the hallway to the open area that contained the kitchen and the living areas, and set the tray on the counter. Then he went to the window and gazed out at the city's skyline. As had happened several times during the past week, the fog that had shrouded the tall buildings in the morning hours had now burned away, and the sun shone down from a brilliantly blue sky. From here he could look north and west toward downtown, toward the damp, foggy streets where he'd pursued Bailey only a few hours earlier. Now, though, it all looked very different.

Still, he could recall Grand Avenue clearly enough, and the battered Porsche that lay on its side, leaking fluids from its engine compartment. Looking at it, any human observer would have said it was beyond repair. However, such an assessment could not take djinn powers into account.

He imagined the car as he had first seen it blazing through L.A.'s empty streets, low and sleek and almost the same sky blue as Bailey's eyes. The growl of its engine, the glint of sunlight on its chrome wheels. Then he imagined that car parked at the curb on the narrow lane outside the building, that same sun shining down on its restored surface.

Yes, there. Smiling, Nasim looked down at the street below, saw the Porsche parked behind a dusty compact SUV that had been sitting there since the Heat transformed the world. Its gleaming blue splendor only made the abandoned vehicle in front of it appear that much more shabby, and he waved a hand, moving the SUV to the next street over so he wouldn't have to look at it.

Pleased with himself, he went to the kitchen to pour himself a glass of wine. The loft's owner had left behind quite a decent collection, and so Nasim had seen no need to summon other vintages to supplement what was already on hand. He drank deeply of the shiraz in his glass, breathed in, and wondered when Bailey would awake next.

He had quite the surprise to show her.

This time, it felt as though she'd been asleep for a while. When she opened her eyes, Bailey saw that the light filtering in from outside was muted and dim. Was it dusk, or that soft purple hour right before dawn, when the world seemed to hold its breath in anticipation of the day to come?

She couldn't know for sure. All she did know was that her mouth felt gummy and nasty, thanks to eating and falling asleep almost immediately afterward, and the ache in her shoulder was more intense than it had been the last time she was awake.

Well, no wonder. She had to strain to see in the darkness, but if the large clock that hung on the wall to her left was correct, then it was a little before six in the morning. And that meant the Percocet Nasim had given her had worn off hours earlier.

Luckily, it looked as though he'd come in sometime while she was dead to the world and set the bottle of pills and a glass of water on the bedside table to her right. Once again she wondered at his kindness. He'd brushed it off by saying he felt responsible for her injuries, but it seemed strange that a djinn would be so concerned about a human's well-being.

She'd have to put that puzzle aside for a time when she felt better. Holding back a groan, she sat up, slid the now-defrosted ice pack off her shoulder, and set it down on the table a little past the water and bottle of Percocet. Her hand shook as she eased off the cap and dropped a pill into her left palm, then reached for the glass of water. It did feel good to have the liquid going down her dry throat, and she took several more swallows before she lay back against the pillows once again.

At the same time, she could feel herself frown.

If she was lying here in splendor on this big king-size bed, then where was Nasim sleeping? She supposed it was possible that the loft had two bedrooms, but if that were the case, wouldn't he have put her in a smaller, secondary room rather than the master?

Because it was clear enough that this had to be the master bedroom, not just because of the expansive closet across the way, but also because of the bathroom off to her right, only dimly visible through more of that frosted glass. It looked very large, almost as big as the bedroom.

Speaking of the bathroom....

All that water was starting to get to her. Although she hated the idea of getting out of her comfortable bed—or Nasim's comfortable bed, more to the point—she knew she had to go.

She clenched her teeth and carefully pushed back the covers, then stood up. The room seemed to spin around her, and she reached down to hold on to the bedside table until the bout of vertigo had passed. Damn, *everything* hurt. Not just her shoulder, but every single goddamn limb and joint in her body.

However, now that she was out of bed, she needed to see this through. Hobbling along like a ninety-year-old with arthritis, she managed to make it into the bathroom and slide the door shut behind her. It wasn't too long before she was back out again, very glad that Nasim hadn't decided it was time for his morning pee as well.

Did djinn even have to pee? They looked so godlike, maybe they were above all bodily functions.

Bailey decided she didn't have the energy to contemplate that particular question. Limping along, she went back to the bed and crawled under the covers again, glad that they hadn't lost all their warmth during her brief absence. The Percocet was starting to kick in, too, smoothing away the little spikes of pain she'd endured during her trip to the bathroom. Good. She might have slept for twelve hours already, but her body felt as though it wanted to sleep for another twelve....

"Bailey."

She cracked an eyelid, saw that bright sun was filtering down the hallway. Clearly, it wasn't going to be another cloudy day, and she was irrationally heartened by that. Then she focused on the man standing by her bedside. Again, he wore jeans and a T-shirt—a short-sleeved one this time, probably a nod to the sunny day. She also realized that his hair was damp and his skin freshly scrubbed and ruddy.

Which meant he'd somehow managed to slip in past her and take a shower while she was conked out. That seemed to indicate the loft only had the one bathroom. She must have been really dead to the world to have slept through all that. If she'd been awake, would she have been able to see him through the frosted glass? Not everything, but at least the outlines of his ridiculously muscled body?

A strange little thrill went through her. She shouldn't be thinking about him like that, not when he was a djinn, and not when she was lying here with a broken collarbone and multiple contusions, her hair a mess and her mouth tasting like the worst morning breath ever.

"What time is it?" she asked, the best thing she could think of to hide her confusion.

Nasim's gaze flicked toward the clock on the wall. "It is almost ten in the morning. I know you needed to sleep, but I thought you might want some food, and some coffee."

Oh, dear lord. Coffee. Bailey had been drinking Starbucks lattes out of cans until she couldn't scrounge any more, but she hadn't had real coffee in months and months. If she could get a decent dose of caffeine circulating in her blood-stream, she thought she might actually start to feel almost human again, despite her injuries.

"Coffee would be good," she said, her tone neutral. She didn't want him to know just how badly she craved the caffeine, even more than food. After all, she'd had the grilled cheese and tomato soup the night before, so it wasn't as though she was as ravenously hungry as she might otherwise be. As she began to struggle to sit up and push her legs over the edge of the bed, he stepped forward, offering her a hand.

"Here."

It was on her lips to say no, but she realized that she would only be doing so to be stubborn, not because she really didn't need his help. In silence, she extended her hand and let him wrap his fingers around hers, raise her up from the bed.

Standing, though, she realized how much of a draft the back of that damn hospital gown let in. Letting go of him, she reached back to hold the stupid thing shut. A small smile touched Nasim's lips.

"I can take care of that," he said, and in the next instant, the hospital gown was gone, replaced by a gray T-shirt and black yoga pants. Everything was soft, comfortable cotton, soothing against her skin, exactly the sort of thing she might have picked out for a leisurely morning...not that she'd had too many of those in her life, since she'd been working at least two jobs ever since she was on her own.

As to how he'd managed to switch out her clothes without jostling her injured arm, Bailey had no idea. The sling was still safely in place, ensuring that her fractured collarbone wouldn't get bumped. Djinn powers, she supposed, just like the ones that had summoned the food she'd eaten the night before. He must have done the same thing to get her into the hospital gown she'd just been wearing a few minutes earlier. The realization made her relax slightly, since now she knew there was no need for him to have manually taken off her clothes.

"This way," he said without waiting for her to comment, and led her out of the bedroom and into the loft's kitchen area.

It was bigger than she'd imagined, although still compact enough. Sitting on the marble countertop was a very expensive-looking stainless coffeemaker; Nasim lifted the carafe from where it sat on the warming plate and poured the dark brew into a white mug, then handed it to her.

"Thank you," she said. Just the aroma on its own was enough to make her feel better, although she knew she'd need to get a few good swallows into her so she could really enjoy the caffeine.

"Cream or sugar?"

"No, I take it black."

This reply elicited a slight lift of his eyebrow, but he didn't comment, only poured coffee into a mug that already sat on the counter. "You're feeling better this morning?"

"Some," she allowed. All right, she still hurt all

over, but those extra four or so hours of sleep really had helped to take the edge off…well, that and the Percocet she'd taken. "Everything still hurts, but not as much as it did yesterday."

"That is good. What would you like for breakfast?"

Good question. Back before the Heat, she hadn't even eaten breakfast half the time, and lately her morning meals had been just another protein bar, possibly supplemented with some dried fruit if she could find it. But if she could have anything she wanted?

"Scrambled eggs and toast," she replied. "Fresh fruit?"

"Simple enough. Why don't you sit down?"

There was a long table that served as both an eating area and a sort of room divider facing the kitchen. Bailey took a chair—the opposite side of the table had a long bench, and she didn't want to struggle with moving that around one-handed— and seated herself, watching as Nasim got a few plates out of the cupboard. Before she could even blink, those plates were filled with golden scrambled eggs, buttered slices of toast, and a pile of fresh fruit that included sliced strawberries, kiwi, and blueberries.

Just looking at the food was enough to make her mouth water. Right then, she wasn't sure if she even cared why Nasim was keeping her around, as long as it meant she could eat like this every day. Maybe at some point she'd have to start worrying about all the calories involved, but she knew she was too thin right now, thanks to the limited diet she'd been stuck with ever since the world ended.

He came over to the table and put the plates down, one in front of her and the other directly across from where she sat. Napkins and knives and forks appeared out of nowhere, and Bailey had to keep herself from startling. Maybe at some point she'd get used to the way he could summon items at will, but right now it was still a little disconcerting.

The bench didn't present any problems for him; he pulled it back a little ways from the table, then sat down opposite her. He seemed to understand that she was still trying to adjust to her surroundings, because he didn't say anything, only picked up his fork and tucked into his scrambled eggs as if it was the most ordinary thing in the world for them to be sharing a meal like this.

For him, maybe it was. Bailey hesitated for a few seconds, then reached down and picked up a piece of toast, then took a bite. Sourdough, just the right crispness, with just the right amount of butter melting into it. Yes, she thought she might be able to get used to this kind of thing.

They ate quietly. Nasim didn't seem all that interested in looking up at her as he ate, which was just fine by her. At least her hair was still pulled into a braid and therefore not a complete and utter disaster, but she hated to think what the rest of her looked like. As if it mattered, though. He was a djinn, and she was a human. For some reason, he'd decided killing her wasn't on today's agenda, but she had no reason to believe that he would have any other kind of interest in her.

Why would he? she thought, shooting a surreptitious glance at him from underneath her eyelashes. *Someone who looks like that could do a lot better than you, even if he wasn't a djinn.*

She wasn't used to having thoughts like that about herself. Most of the time, she did pretty well when it came to male attention. Actually, it could be a real pain in the ass, although she hadn't been above using her looks to provide some extra leverage when necessary. It was her long legs and long blonde hair that had gotten her that first modeling gig at the car show, after all. Yes, just a local thing, nothing fancy like the international auto show they'd held every year at the L.A. Convention Center, but if she hadn't worked that one gig, she would never have met Oscar, who owned a custom car shop in El Monte and who, after talking with her for a few minutes, had realized a keen automotive brain lurked behind those big blue eyes…and who offered her a job on the spot.

At first she'd thought it was only a ploy to get into her pants. So what if he was thirty years older than she, heavyset and not all that attractive? Men tended to have an inflated view of their own looks, while most of the girls Bailey had known seemed intent on dissecting every single flaw they possessed, whether it was boobs that were too small or hair that wasn't thick enough or eyes that weren't the exact right shade of blue, or whatever. But her body wasn't what Oscar had wanted. He wanted to see what she could do with a set of wrenches, and after she expertly re-cored the radiator on a '68 Chevelle he was restoring, he knew she wasn't talking out both sides of her mouth. She'd gone to work for him, part time at first, and probably would have still been there when the Heat swept over the world...if it hadn't been for Diego.

Her mouth turned down, and at once Nasim asked, "Is there something wrong with the food?"

"No," Bailey said hastily, returning to her neglected eggs. Somehow, they were still nice and toasty warm, even though eggs were notorious for going cold if you even looked at them the wrong way. More djinn magic, she supposed. "I was just thinking."

"About?"

No way was she going to tell him about Diego, about the relationship that eventually soured Oscar on her and led him to fire her, even though she knew she did great work. She might have been good enough to rebuild a carburetor, but she definitely wasn't good enough for Oscar's only son.

"Cars," she said, the first thing that popped into her head. Well, that wasn't even technically a lie.

To her surprise, Nasim smiled. "I have something to show you, once you're done with breakfast."

Was that a promise or a threat? It was hard to say, although the djinn looked cheerful enough. Again, she wondered whether the nice act was all just an elaborate ploy to get her to keep her guard down, so he might attack her when she least expected it. With the shape she was in, it wasn't as though she could fight back very effectively.

That didn't mean she wouldn't try, though.

"Okay," she said, and put down her fork and reached for her coffee. A few large swallows made her feel a bit better about life. Not completely better, but enough that she could finish the rest of the food on her plate, grateful at least for a full stomach. Once she was done, she pushed the empty dish away from her and folded the napkin —cloth, not paper—on the tabletop. "So what did you want to show me?"

Nasim set aside his own napkin and got up from the bench. "Come over to the window."

That request didn't sound too frightening—unless he intended to push her out that same window. Telling herself that djinn had much more efficient ways of killing humans, Bailey rose from her seat and followed him over to the window in question, which provided a stunning view of downtown Los Angeles. Her estimate of the loft's probable cost rose a few notches. You didn't get views like that without laying down some serious cash.

Still, there wasn't much else for her to see. She turned toward Nasim. "And?"

"Look down."

Mouth pursed, she moved a little closer to the window and gazed down at the street below. A flash of familiar blue immediately caught her eye.

No, it couldn't be—

"Is that—?"

"Yes," Nasim said smoothly. "I retrieved your vehicle and repaired it, then brought it here."

"I—" Bailey didn't know what the hell she should say in response. Yes, the djinn had already shown her that he had all sorts of amazing powers, but never in a million years would she have guessed that he could simply snap his fingers and fix her totaled Porsche. That car had been creamed. It should have been towed away on a flatbed truck…if there had been anyone left to perform that kind of service. "Um…thank you."

"You're welcome." He looked down at the car for a few more seconds, then shifted so he faced her. "You don't seem all that happy about it. It seemed to me that the car was important to you, and that's why I fixed it."

"I am happy," she protested. "I just—" Bailey had to break off there, because she wasn't sure what she'd meant to say. "I guess it's just hard to look at when I know I won't be able to drive it for a long time."

"Then you need to focus on healing as quickly as you can," he said.

Well, she couldn't argue with that suggestion. She gazed at him, trying to see if there had been any kind of subtext to his words. As far as she could tell, there wasn't, but she barely knew him. Right now he just looked sort of thoughtful, as if he was also trying to figure her out.

Good luck with that, she thought. *I've lived with myself all these years and haven't been too successful at it.*

The silence was awkward, but Bailey didn't know what to say to fill it. Instead, she turned her attention to the window once again, to the gleaming blue car parked down on the street below. She itched to get behind the wheel again, even though she knew she couldn't drive. She couldn't do anything with this goddamn broken collarbone.

A sudden notion occurred to her, one so crazy, she wasn't sure she should even voice it aloud. Then again, Nasim had basically just proved that there didn't seem to be much outside the scope of his abilities.

Without looking at him, she said, "You healed my car. Why can't you heal me?"

Dead silence. This time she had to risk a quick glance at Nasim, just so she could see how her suggestion had been received. His brows were pulled together, and he gave a quick shake of his head.

"That's not possible."

"Why not?"

"My people have no need of healers. Our injuries heal quickly, and we never become ill."

"That's not what I asked."

Again he was quiet. It looked as though he was thinking over what she'd said, trying to find fault with it.

"What's the worst that could happen?" Bailey inquired. "I mean, really?"

"I could hurt you."

"I'm already hurt," she pointed out.

He huffed out a breath. "I doubt it would work."

"But maybe it will."

For a second, he didn't respond. Then his shoulders lifted. "Very well. I will try. Stand still."

She nodded and waited, standing as quietly as she could. Nasim reached toward her with one hand. He hesitated, eyes narrowed, then nodded to himself. Very carefully, his fingers slipped under the strap of the sling she wore, under the neckline of her T-shirt.

His fingers were very warm. Bailey hadn't been expecting that, probably because she'd been so out of it the last time he'd touched her, she couldn't remember much of the experience. It was an odd sensation, to hold herself completely still as his palm flattened itself against her collarbone. Another of those strange little thrills worked its way through her body. This djinn was touching her, the warmth of his flesh feeling like the world's most intimate hot pad.

It was *too* intimate, but she'd coaxed him into this, so now she had no choice but to remain where she was and hope that his magic or whatever it was really could do more than just summon food and repair totaled sports cars. Bailey breathed in, making sure her gaze never met his. Right then, she wasn't quite sure what she would do if she allowed herself to fall into those blue, blue depths.

And then, so gently that she hardly noticed what was happening at first, the pain receded, ocean waters pulling away from a harsh and rocky shore. Not all the pain, true; she could still feel the twinge from the gash in her forehead, the various aches and throbs from the bumps and bruises all over her body. But the worst pain, the dull, gnawing ache in her shoulder, that was gone.

Although she'd told herself not to make eye contact, she couldn't help but look up into his face. Those deep azure eyes caught hers, and she pulled in a breath. "You did it," she whispered.

He didn't move his hand away. "You're sure?"

"Yes. You fixed the break. I can feel it."

Very gently, he pushed down on her collarbone. If the fracture had still been there, even that mild pressure probably would have been enough to make her gasp in agony. But although the flesh around the break was still tender, the underlying problem was gone. "Did that hurt?"

"No."

Nasim's expression was almost as wondering as hers must have been. "I had no idea. I would never—well, I had never thought to attempt such a thing."

"You probably had no reason to heal a human before."

"True." He hesitated for a moment, then said, "Well, if you are healed, then you have no need of that sling."

"Perfect." Bailey reached up and undid the

Velcro at the back of her neck. Yes, there was some muscle stiffness, but that should go away soon enough. And she thought of the perfect way to help it along. She shot a grateful smile at Nasim. "I guess this means I can take a shower now."

FIVE

ALTHOUGH HE REMAINED OUT IN THE LIVING room area, Nasim fancied he could hear the sound of water rushing in the shower enclosure. It was quite a large space, with more than enough room for two people to stand under the enormous shower heads and let the water rain down, but he'd known better than to suggest that kind of an activity to Bailey. She would never allow such a liberty.

Besides, he'd already showered.

He sat on the couch and watched the sunlight stream through the living room window and touch his hand, which lay palm up on his thigh. It was hard to believe that that same hand had just touched Bailey, had somehow sent its power within to heal the fractured bone beneath her smooth skin.

But it had. Or rather, he had.

The process had not been so very different from what he had done to repair her car. He had visualized the break within the bone, imagined his power surrounding the tiny fracture and smoothing over the break. It hadn't been impossible, or even difficult.

And now Bailey was free of the sling, and in the shower. Frankly, she'd needed a good cleaning-up; although she wasn't outright dirty, had probably used bottled water to keep herself as clean as possible, her hair had been a bit greasy, and the deodorant she'd worn hadn't been quite enough to prevent him from noticing that it had probably been months since she'd had a proper shower or bath.

Shower, he guessed. She didn't seem much like a bath person.

It was hard not to think about her in the shower, about the water running over her slender body and soaking her pale gold hair. In fact, the more he tried not to think about it, the more his thoughts dwelled on how lovely she was, and then his body began to respond.

No. She'd given absolutely no indication that she had any interest in him, other than as the person who'd just miraculously healed her. Now that she was better—despite her other, much more minor injuries—would she get in her car and drive away?

He didn't want that to happen. For one thing, he found he liked talking to Bailey, despite her often brittle responses to his questions. Although seeking companionship certainly had not been his intention when he decided to hunt her down, he realized that his previous existence had been quite a lonely one, and she somehow filled a gap he hadn't even known was there. He still did not know much about her, but he had the impression that the world had not treated her very well. Oddly—for he would never have called himself a tender man, not at all—he found he wanted to take care of her. He'd actually looked forward to nursing her back to health, but it seemed a lengthy convalescence was no longer in order.

Which meant he needed to think of some other reason to keep her around.

A dangerous game, to be sure. He knew just as well as the rest of his kind that fraternizing with humans was not allowed in this new world. They were Chosen, or they were prey; there was no in between. He'd been here in this borrowed loft for more than a week, and so far the elders had ignored him, hadn't appeared on his doorstep to inform him that he needed to return to Napa. They must have been occupied elsewhere, which suited him just fine. Luckily, they were not gods, were not omnipotent. Whatever the elders might be up to at the moment, it seemed that he'd been left to his own devices, at least for now.

This territory wasn't his.

Bailey wasn't his.

But he wanted them both.

He'd first pursued her on the streets of Los Angeles because he'd wanted the challenge, had wanted to succeed where so many others of his kind had failed. Now he realized that Bailey still presented just as much of a challenge, if of a different sort.

Was he up to that challenge?

He supposed he would have to find out.

The sound of the water in the bathroom stopped. Nasim forced himself to remain where he was, as much as he would have liked to catch a glimpse of Bailey as she stepped out of the shower. Strange how he wanted to indulge himself in something he knew was completely improper. She must be having more of an effect on him than he'd thought, and that wouldn't do. He needed to stay in control.

While he hadn't known much of human women and their needs when it came to toiletries and such—the previous owner of this loft had clearly been male—Nasim had been able to gather what he hoped was a selection of items Bailey could use when getting ready, lotions and products for her hair, makeup and brushes and whatnot. It seemed he had chosen well, because she was smiling when she finally emerged from the bedroom, fully dressed and combing out her long, damp hair.

Or possibly she was happy because she had had a hot shower, and her shoulder was no longer injured.

She came into the living room and sat down on one of the chairs that faced the sofa where Nasim had been waiting for her. Now she did look truly beautiful, clean and shiny, wearing just a hint of makeup. The gash on her forehead had been covered by a bandage, but it couldn't mar her fresh-scrubbed loveliness.

Because he could tell she was not a woman given to frills, the clothes he'd provided were simple enough—slim-fitting jeans, a sleeveless top in a clear blue to complement her eyes, flat shoes. Even though the clothing was plain, she still looked beautiful in it, possibly because there was nothing to draw attention away from the symmetry of her features or the slender graceful-ness of her body.

"How do you do it?" she asked.

"Do what?"

"All this." One hand waved in the general direction of the master suite, but perhaps she meant the loft as a whole. "Electricity and running water. *Hot* running water."

"It's simple enough," Nasim replied. "I use a small fraction of my powers to keep those necessities operating. Not even a djinn wants a cold shower."

Bailey stared at him for a second, and then she chuckled. "No, I guess wanting warm water is kind of universal. What made you choose this place, anyway?"

"You," he said honestly, and her eyes widened.

"What do you mean?"

"I came here to pursue you, to see if I could do better than the other djinn who'd sought to track you down. It made more sense to live someplace near the area where you'd been spotted."

"There are plenty of other lofts and apartments in downtown, though."

"True." He shrugged and snapped his fingers, and a pair of glasses filled with ice water appeared on the distressed-wood coffee table. "I did not want to be up in a high-rise."

"Afraid of heights?" she asked, and he realized she was teasing him, because of course she must have seen him pursuing her from the air before he realized he needed to meet her on her own terms.

"Not exactly. I felt it would help me more to be closer to street level. I found these lofts, and this one suited me. So here we are."

This comment seemed to disturb her, because she shifted where she sat and gazed past him, to the window that framed the tall buildings of L.A.'s downtown. Then she took a breath, crossed her arms, and met his eyes squarely. "Yes, here we are. But what does that mean, exactly?"

Nasim wasn't sure whether he was intimidated by her directness…or impressed by it. "I suppose it means whatever you want it to mean."

One side of her mouth twitched slightly, but he thought it was from irritation rather than amusement. "That's not an answer."

"It is, even it's not one you wanted to hear."

A gust of breath escaped her lips, and she got up from where she sat and went back over to the window. This time she glanced down at the street, possibly to reassure herself that the Porsche was still parked there. Her back to him, she said, "Will you let me go?"

He supposed he should have anticipated such a request, but it still surprised him…and disappointed him as well. Almost since he'd met her, he'd been struggling with his attraction to Bailey, and some part of him had clearly expected the feeling to be mutual. Then again, she had no idea that humans and djinn could be intimate. She must have believed that he viewed her as a captured adversary, and nothing more. As far as he could tell, she hadn't gone farther west than the edges of downtown, and so she had no idea that a community of djinn and their human Chosen had been established in the area known as Bel-Air.

However, he knew he must be careful in his reply, for he did not want to frighten her—if that was even possible. She'd dealt with him almost as an equal, despite her position as something somewhere between a houseguest and a captive. Once again, he had the sense of tragedies buried and forgotten, except where they might help make her stronger.

"If I did," he said, "what then?"

Now she turned back toward him, clearly somewhat startled that he hadn't dismissed her question out of hand. "I suppose I'd go back to what I was doing before. Surviving."

"That's all you want from your life?"

Her pretty mouth curled in an ironic smile. "What else is there?"

Nasim got up from the couch and came toward her. Judging by the way her body went still, he could tell she was poised to flee, even if she knew deep down that she wouldn't be able to get very far. "I could give you much more than that."

Once again her arms crossed. Her entire slender frame seemed to radiate a clear message of *Stay away*, and so he made sure to stop before he got too close. Chin lifted and eyes narrowed, she said, "Like what?"

If only he could show her, could bend down and press his lips against hers. However, he sensed that would be exactly the wrong thing to do. The only way to get close to her would be to gradually chip away at the wall she'd built around herself… if such a thing was even possible. For now, he thought it probably was best to open her mind a bit.

"Just about anything you wanted," he replied. "Did you like the Ferrari I was driving?"

She didn't exactly sniff, but he could tell Bailey wasn't impressed by the question. "I like my Porsche. We know each other."

Well, at least he had done one thing right. Clearly, she was attached to the car, even if she could have had her pick of the most extravagant vehicles the former world had once offered. "What else have you wanted, something you knew would probably always be out of reach for you?"

Instead of her blue eyes lighting up in antici-pation, she grew even more shuttered, if such a thing was possible. "Nothing."

Nasim found that difficult to believe. "Nothing at all?"

"I said nothing, and I meant it," she stated flatly. "And I'm really not into games. Either you're going to let me go, or you're not. Which is it? I want to know where we stand."

Irritation swirled within him, but he did his best to push it away. After all, he'd wanted a challenge, something to engage his mind and his spirit, and Bailey was definitely that. A sudden notion occurred to him, and he did his best to repress a smile. He didn't want her to see how pleased he was with himself. "I'll let you go, if—"

"If?" she interrupted, arms still crossed.

"If you race me. You win, and I'll let you go. More than that, I'll make sure you're stocked with supplies and will watch over you all the way to Los Alamos…or I can take you there djinn-style. Whichever you want." He knew Los Alamos was the only settlement of non-Chosen humans left in the world. It was also the only place where Bailey could be safe. If she wouldn't stay here with him, then at least she should have some kind of sanctuary.

He'd expected her to ask why he would guide her to someplace in New Mexico, but she remained silent, obviously contemplating his offer. Perhaps she had some knowledge of the survivors in Los Alamos. How, he wasn't sure, but possibly someone in the group there had managed to get out a message before the world went dark.

At last she said, "And if I lose?"

"Then you'll stay here with me."

She didn't blink. "What does that mean, exactly?"

"What do you think it means?"

A long silence. Her eyes scanned his face, at last flaring wider with a sort of wary shock. "Do you mean humans and djinn...?" And she stopped there, looking awkward for the first time since he'd met her.

"Yes," he replied simply.

"Jesus." Another pause, and then she asked, "Then why kill us?"

A good question, one he wasn't sure he could answer adequately. Djinn had widely varying opinions of the human race, although a good many of them believed mortals were a scourge on the planet that should be eliminated, a belief that had led to the development of the deadly fever that killed so many of them. He hadn't subscribed to that belief, but unfortunately, the minority to which he belonged was small enough that they had never been able to dissuade the rest of their people from carrying out their deadly plans. With a lift of his shoulders, he said, "I suppose one might ask why humans could enslave other humans, murder them, abuse them...but also lie with them and bear children with them. These things are not always so simple."

Her lips pressed together. Obviously, she hadn't much cared for his reply. "I know we did terrible things to each other. But it isn't the same. Djinn are different from humans. We're not the same race."

"No, we're not," he agreed. "But we are very close. Close enough to be intimate, close enough to create life together."

That was obviously something she hadn't wanted to hear. Now her crossed arms appeared more as if she was hugging herself, trying to keep unwanted truths from penetrating the armor she'd created for herself for most of her life. When she spoke, though, her voice was hard, almost brittle. "I hope you're not saying you want to have little half-djinn babies with me."

His daydreams hadn't progressed quite that far, although Nasim thought that he and Bailey would have beautiful children together, if the situation allowed. Still, first things first. "Not precisely. Or rather, I was thinking more of the activities that precede conception."

She swallowed. "Let me get this straight, then. We race. I win, I go free and you see me safely to the human community in New Mexico. You win, I have to stay here as your sex toy."

"I wouldn't have put it so baldly," he replied, "but basically, yes."

Once again, she was quiet for a moment. Then she said, "Best two out of three."

He blinked at her. "What?"

"We race three times," she responded, speaking slowly, as if to a child or someone with thick wits. "The person who wins two out of three races wins the bet. I don't want something like this riding on a single race."

"Fair enough."

"Okay." She pulled in a breath before she extended her hand to him. He took it, felt how cold and thin her fingers were. A slight tremor went through her, and she said, "You have yourself a bet, Nasim al-Jibril."

This was crazy. Had she really just agreed to race for her...well, "virtue" was a bit strong, considering she'd given up her virginity years ago, but....

Her body. That's what Nasim wanted, crazy as it sounded to her. For more than half a year, she'd told herself that djinn had to be entirely separate from mankind, no matter how similar the two races might look. But now he'd told her that humans and djinn apparently did the nasty from time to time, even if it didn't seem as though such couplings were exactly a common occurrence.

Well, at least now she didn't have to feel quite so strange about those random lustful thoughts she'd had about him. He must have been thinking basically the same thing about her. He hadn't tried anything, though, and God only knew that he could have.

Nasim was smiling at her now. Did he think he was going to win, just because he'd succeeded in making her panic and crash her car? She was hip to his game now; that wasn't going to happen again.

"Any rules?" he asked.

Thinking furiously, she replied, "Three different courses. I'll choose the first and third ones, and you can choose the second."

He nodded, rubbing his chin in an abstracted way. "Anything else?"

"We drive the same cars. They can be Ferraris or Porsches or whatever you want, but we need to race in identical vehicles so no one has an unfair advantage."

"That's easy enough. I'll choose for the first and third races, and you can choose for the second."

Wily of him. This way, they'd be selecting the vehicles for the other person's course, and so couldn't select something specifically designed for straightaway acceleration, or that was better for taking corners at speed. "No problem," she said. "Otherwise, standard street racing rules—no deliberately crashing into the other person's vehicle, no aftermarket equipment that we haven't both agreed on first."

"What is aftermarket equipment?"

It was kind of nice to know that there were gaps in Nasim's knowledge of human culture and technology. "Anything you install after you buy the car from a dealer. Blowers, nitrous, upgraded exhaust, premium brake pads—"

The djinn held up a hand. "I understand. Stock vehicles, like what I would take from a dealership."

"Right." And with his pick of all the abandoned vehicles in all the luxury car dealers in the Los Angeles area, Bailey could only imagine what he might come up with. "And...." She let the word trail off, not sure of the best way to state her final request. Nasim had seemed agreeable enough so far—probably because all her stipulations amused him in a way, since he would always have the upper hand when dealing with a human—but she also didn't want to push him.

"And?" he asked, one eyebrow lifting slightly.

"I need to stay someplace else. One of the other lofts in the building."

"Why?" He appeared genuinely curious.

"Because it's weird sleeping in your bed. Where did you sleep last night, anyway? On the couch?"

"Yes," he replied.

Well, his answer told her that djinn actually did sleep. Nasim didn't appear angered by her request, only a bit puzzled. Feeling encouraged, Bailey went on, "I just think it's better if you have your place back. This building is full of empty lofts, right? I can take the one next door. I won't try to get away."

"I know you won't," he said, "because we've already agreed on a bet, and I know you wouldn't go back on your word like that. Having you next door would be easier in terms of making sure you have power and hot water."

His words almost made her feel guilty, as though he thought of her as some kind of honor-able person when she'd given him absolutely no reason to believe such a thing. All right, she'd certainly never set out to purposely cheat or hurt anyone, but at the same time, she wasn't sure she deserved such a high opinion.

Rather than argue, though, she only nodded. "Sounds good. Why don't we go over and take a look?"

"Very well."

He sounded resigned. Had she hurt his feel-ings by asking to stay in the loft next door? Bailey tried to tell herself she shouldn't be worried about his feelings, not when they'd basically just made a bet that involved whether he'd end up sleeping with her, but it was hard not to feel a little guilty when he'd healed her wounds and fed her and let her take that amazing shower…and repaired her Porsche for her.

Toughen up, honey, she told herself as she followed Nasim to the loft that would be her new crash space—for a little while, anyway. *Otherwise, you might as well give in now and let him fuck you.*

No way. There were probably worse fates…a *lot* worse fates, considering how gorgeous he was…but her pride was involved now. If she ended up going to bed with him, it would be because he'd beaten her fair and square.

Assuming he didn't cheat, of course. Somehow, though, Bailey didn't think he would. His actions had already proved that he had his own personal sense of honor, even if it didn't always match up with hers.

"Here you are," he said, laying fingers on the doorknob and letting the door swing inward. She hadn't seen him use any kind of key, but since he was able to heal broken bones with a touch and snap his fingers to summon her food, she realized he probably didn't need a key to get in.

This loft looked bigger than the one Nasim had taken for his own, and probably was more expensive back when those things mattered, but Bailey liked his better. There, the designer had used some warmth and whimsy to choose the furniture, whereas this place was cold and industrial, white walls and ceiling, polished concrete floor. The sofas were gray, as was the area rug beneath them. Still, she wasn't staying here to get all warm and fuzzy. She was doing this because she thought it was probably better to put a little distance between her and Nasim.

"Great," she said, hoping she sounded at least a little enthusiastic. "This'll be fine. I just need to go back and grab the stuff in the bathroom you got for me—"

"No need," he cut in, his words now a bit short, as though he was finally starting to lose his patience with her. "Everything is already here, along with a few changes of clothing."

"Oh, well...thanks, I guess." Feeling nonplussed, Bailey added, "I guess I'll just go out and choose the course for tomorrow's race, then. If that's okay."

"It's fine," Nasim said. "There are no other djinn in the area, so it should be safe enough. Is there anything else you need?"

"Traffic cones," she replied promptly. "I can use them to mark the course—unless you think that'll be too conspicuous."

"As I said, there are no other djinn around to see what we're doing. Go ahead and use them to lay out the course. What time did you want to race tomorrow?"

"Um...noon?" Bailey responded, a bit startled

by the question. Sure, she'd asked for separate accommodations, but she supposed that she would still be spending some time with Nasim between now and the race. For one thing, what was she supposed to eat for dinner? It wouldn't be the first time she'd gone to bed hungry, but with the race coming up....

"I will come get you at noon, then," Nasim said. "I've also put some food in the refrigerator for you. Have a good afternoon and evening."

He sort of nodded at her, then went to the door and let himself out. It wasn't quite as rude as blinking himself away, but Bailey found herself staring at that closed door, wondering how much she'd angered him by requesting a separate place to sleep.

Well, it couldn't be helped now. She sure as hell wasn't going to walk over to Nasim's loft and beg his forgiveness, not when she hadn't done anything wrong in the first place. He could just suck it up.

Frowning, she went over to the fridge. At least Nasim had no intention of starving her—she found a frozen pizza, one of those kinds you just had to stick in the oven to heat up, neatly labeled containers of Chinese takeout, a half-carton of eggs. Once upon a time, she might have wondered where the hell you could get Chinese takeout after the apocalypse, but obviously, these minor details weren't an issue for a djinn.

She got out a container of lo mein and went to the microwave, mind already working at the problem of where she'd set up the next day's race. If she kept herself busy with logistics, then she wouldn't have to wonder what she would do if the impossible happened and she somehow lost.

SIX

Nasim stared at the wall that separated his loft from the one where Bailey was staying, and tried not to scowl. Actually, hers had been a perfectly reasonable request. His place had just the one bedroom, and it was clear that the only way the two of them would end up sharing a bed was if he somehow managed to win two out of the three races they had planned. Even so, he couldn't quite push his irritation away. He knew it had seeped out during his last exchange with Bailey, and he was sure she must have noticed.

She was gone now, taking the Porsche so she could scout locations for tomorrow's race. Although it would have been easy enough to follow her, to spy on her as she set up the course, he wouldn't allow himself to do such a thing. If he won, he wanted it to be because his driving skills had outmatched hers, and not because he had used his djinn powers to gain an unfair advantage.

However, just because he had vowed not to follow her, that didn't mean he couldn't go up to the rooftop deck and make sure the coast was still clear. It was a simple but luxurious space, with a rectangular swimming pool, several rows of chaise longues, and a covered patio area with groupings of armchairs and tables, perfect for sitting out on a warm night and watching the stars. Once upon a time, stargazing would have been difficult here, thanks to all the lights of Los Angeles outshining everything but the brightest constellations, but their interference was no longer a worry, obviously.

Nasim had thought he might bring Bailey up here, but that particular activity would have to wait until they had settled this bet. He had no doubt in his mind that he would win, that he would be able to enjoy many starlit nights here with her. Yes, she was a skilled driver, but her human reflexes couldn't begin to match his. Djinn were faster, stronger, had quicker reactions. She had done very well to survive on her own for so long, and yet he thought she would understand soon enough that losing to a djinn was not a shameful thing.

The skies above L.A. remained clear, not a cloud to mar that serene blue expanse. He could not sense any other djinn anywhere near—not that he had expected to. There were those who dwelled in Bel-Air, and a few who had been given lands to the east of here, but none of those djinn had any reason to come near downtown. It was now a no man's land, which suited Nasim's plans perfectly.

Even so, he let his gaze sweep over the city's high-rises and warehouses and office buildings, scanning the music complex toward the northeast where Bailey had crashed the Porsche, all the way to the nearly derelict structures that lined what used to be Skid Row. If any of that area's unfortunates had survived the Heat, they wouldn't have stood a chance against the djinn reavers that came afterward.

All was still. He wasn't able to catch a glimpse of Bailey's sky-blue Porsche, which was just as well. This way, he could honestly claim that he had no advance knowledge of the course she had chosen. However, he could guess well enough. She excelled at slaloming through the city's empty streets, pushing her vehicle to the limit as she took sharp corners at speeds that would have made a less skilled driver surely crash. He had no doubt that she would pick just such a course because it would showcase her talents and put him at a disadvantage.

Which meant he needed to select vehicles that would work well on that type of track. The Porsche was an obvious choice, but Bailey was already far too familiar with the vehicle, and that would give her an additional advantage.

She'd sneered at the Ferrari, but Nasim found himself reconsidering the vehicle. It had handled extremely well, besides having such a brutally efficient engine that even he, a djinn, had grinned as he muscled the thing down Grand Avenue in pursuit of Bailey's Porsche. Yes, he thought the Ferrari 488 would do very well.

He had gotten the car off the lot at a dealership in Beverly Hills, but that had been a little too close to the Bel-Air community of djinn and Chosen for his comfort. Having another vehicle of the exact same make and model disappear within a short period of time might draw their attention.

Luckily, there was a dealership in Newport Beach, less than a hundred miles away. And that dealership had the same vehicle as the one Nasim had taken from the Beverly Hills lot, only in a beautiful deep greenish metallic blue that he thought Bailey would like, considering the sky color of the Porsche she loved so much. He called the Ferrari to him, parking it under the loft complex next to his blood-colored sports car. As far as he knew, Bailey had no idea the tuck-under garage even existed, so he thought the car should remain a surprise until he brought it out the following day.

That task managed, he went back downstairs to his loft, which already felt strangely empty, now that he knew Bailey wouldn't be returning here. No matter; in a few days, she would be his. Then the only real decision would be whether to enjoy their illicit rendezvous here in Los Angeles for a while longer, or whether he should take her back to Napa. The place he had been given there was very beautiful, and perhaps she would enjoy it as a change from the cement corridors of downtown L.A.

He fetched himself a glass of wine and wandered into the bedroom, then trailed his hand over the bed, now neatly made up, no trace that Bailey had slept there the night before.

Soon, he thought.

She drove through L.A.'s empty streets, body tense, even though Nasim had assured her there were no other djinn around and that she would be safe from pursuit. Unfortunately, old habits died hard.

So many choices. The way Los Angeles Street

and Hope Street intersected was insanely confusing; that might be a good place to gain an advantage, because even a djinn might have a hard time parsing the direction of travel while moving at top speed. They could go old school and head east out of downtown by way of the Second Street tunnel, immortalized in way too many movies to count.

Or....

Nasim would be expecting her to set up a twisty course because she was good at that kind of driving. Wouldn't it be better to do something completely different, throw him off-balance? He'd probably choose cars that were good at hunkering down on the corners rather than hauling ass in a straight line, which meant if she picked someplace to drag race rather than slalom, it really would be down to their reflexes and how fast they could be off the line.

Hmm.

She dropped down to Eighth Street and followed it west until she got to the on-ramp for the 110 Freeway. Here, just as on downtown's streets, the abandoned cars had been pushed off to the side. By the djinn, obviously, although Bailey didn't know for sure why they'd cleared the highway. Had they thought she might use this route to try to escape them, and so cleared it so she'd be easier to spot from above? Maybe.

It really didn't matter. What mattered was that

all four northbound lanes were wide open,
heading in a straight line toward the interchange
with the 101 Freeway on the northeast side of
downtown. And it wasn't that long a stretch,
about a mile and a half. Of course, when you were
stuck in some of the world's worst traffic on that
part of the freeway, that mile and a half felt more
like five hundred miles, but traffic jams were a
thing of the past now, just like so many other
relics of the world before the djinn came.

They could start here, just after the on-ramp
dumped them onto the freeway. The end point
would be where the 110 cut under the 101. There
wouldn't be any finish lines or checkered flags, but
she'd found a dozen small traffic cones crammed
into the Porsche's trunk—placed there by Nasim,
she guessed—and they would serve well enough
to mark the race's endpoint. She wouldn't set
them across the asphalt, but rather in two groups
of three on either side of the freeway. That should
be a visible enough finish line.

Confident that she'd chosen a good venue,
Bailey continued along the empty freeway, then
stopped where the 101 crossed on top of the 110.
A wary glance up at the sky—which remained
empty, just as Nasim had promised her—and then
she climbed out of the Porsche, retrieved the
traffic cones from the trunk, and put them where
the shadow of the overpass traced its way across

the ground. Once she had completed that task, she got back in her car and drove a little ways further, waiting until she could exit a bit north of Chinatown, then loop back around and head south. Maybe it was stupid to follow those pre-ordained entrances and exits when all she really had to do was turn the Porsche and go back the way she'd come, but something felt strange about driving the wrong way on the freeway, even if there was no one else around to share the road.

Altogether, her explorations had taken her about an hour. When she got back to the loft complex on the east side of downtown and parked on the street out front, she didn't see any sign of Nasim. Then again, why would she? If he'd been standing at the lobby entrance, waiting for her, she would have thought that kind of behavior clingy and a little strange.

Still, it felt weird to go into the building, walk past the bank of mailboxes in the lobby, and go up the stairs to the second floor where both their borrowed lofts were located. There was an elevator, but she doubted he would bother to expend the extra energy to keep it running. Besides, after driving for an hour, it felt good to stretch her legs by walking up the stairs.

The door to her loft was unlocked. Good thing, since Nasim hadn't given her a key. When she closed the door behind her, Bailey wondered whether she should bother with the deadbolt. Probably not; the djinn next door had already shown her that locks weren't any kind of a deterrent.

She set the key fob for the Porsche down on the dining table and went into the small but functional kitchen area. There was a pitcher of cold water in the refrigerator, so she poured some for herself. Since she'd snacked on lo mein before she went out, she didn't need to eat anything for a while.

Which meant she had a lot of empty afternoon and evening hours to fill up. There wasn't a clock anywhere she could see, so she didn't know exactly what time it was. Judging by the angle of the sun overhead, though, she guessed it couldn't be much later than one o'clock.

The months she'd spent running hadn't left a lot of room for boredom. Now, though, Bailey realized she didn't have much to do with herself until her race with Nasim almost twenty-four hours from now. Would it seem completely desperate if she went over and knocked on his door?

Probably.

There was a low bookcase in the living room. She walked over to it and perused its contents, even though she'd never been much of a reader. What she found wasn't exactly interesting, either

—a pristine row of *Architectural Digest* magazines that looked as though they'd never been read, some pretentious-looking hardbacks with abstract images on the covers and even more abstract blurbs on the dust covers, a few reference books.

Great. Right then she would've killed for access to the internet. At least then she could have researched cars, tried to guess what kind of vehicles Nasim had chosen for their confrontation tomorrow.

Failing the internet or any kind of decent reading material, she took her glass of water and decided to go exploring. From the outside, the building appeared to have five stories. Since she was already on the second floor, that wasn't much of a climb.

Bailey went to the stairwell and headed up, spurred on by the promise offered by the signs posted there that announced a swimming pool and roof access. Sure enough, when she emerged from the stairs, she saw a neat rectangular pool glinting in the sun, several rows of inviting loungers, and a little covered patio area off to one side.

Of course, what she also saw was Nasim, lying on one of those chaise longues, dark sunglasses covering his eyes, torso bare to the bright sun overhead.

Damn.

It was hard not to stare. He hadn't put on suntan oil or anything that she could tell, but his skin still seemed to glisten in the sunlight. Maybe that was just sweat.

Since the last thing she wanted was for him to think she'd been standing there and gawking at him, she cleared her throat as she approached and said, "Hey."

Nasim sat up, although he didn't remove his sunglasses. "Hello, Bailey. Beautiful day, isn't it?"

He seemed so relaxed, whereas she felt like a bundle of nerves. Stupid, because it wasn't as though she hadn't seen plenty of half-naked guys during her career, even ones whose bodies were almost as good as Nasim's.

The key word being "almost."

She sat down on the lounger next to him. "Yes, it's nice." And damn, didn't that sound stupid, too. This wasn't some garden party or something where she needed to make small talk. "I picked the spot for our race tomorrow."

"Good."

His tone was so neutral, she couldn't quite tell whether he was still annoyed with her for vacating his loft. Hating the awkward little silence that fell after he uttered that one word, she went on, "How did you want to work that, exactly? Follow me to the starting point?"

"You can meet me in the lobby at noon," he

said. "I'll take you to your car, and then you can drive to where we'll race."

"Sounds good. I guess I'll see you then."

Bailey began to turn so she could leave, and was startled to feel him reach out and grasp her hand, stopping her, although he let go almost immediately when she paused. "Why hurry off?" he asked. "It's a beautiful day. Stay here and enjoy the sunlight."

Its warmth did feel good. During her months of running and hiding, she hadn't had much of an opportunity to let herself bask in Southern California's famous sunshine. Still, she felt as though she should make at least a token protest. "I'm going to fry in this sun."

Before she could even blink, a bottle of sunscreen dropped into her hand. She clutched the plastic container, wrapping her fingers around it before it could fall to the concrete. In her other hand was a wad of black fabric. Puzzled, she tucked the sunscreen under one arm so she could untangle the fabric and see what it was.

Not that there was much to untangle, as it turned out. What she held was a skimpy bikini bottom and even skimpier top.

"You expect me to wear this?" she asked.

He shrugged, even as the jeans he wore disappeared, replaced by a pair of dark blue swim trunks. Not a Speedo, thank God, but still. Now she could see that his legs were just as heavily muscled as his shoulders and arms...not that she had expected anything else. He pushed his sunglasses up on his nose. "It seems a shame to waste that swimming pool."

"There's no place to change," Bailey pointed out, since she felt as though he was trying to bulldoze her, and she wasn't about to simply roll over for him.

Even though Nasim had just adjusted his sunglasses, he still removed them so he could give her an ironic glance. "That's really not an issue, you know."

Oh, shit. Since he'd magically switched out his jeans for swim trunks and had made new clothes appear on her just the day before, she knew all he had to do was snap his fingers to remove the jeans and top she wore now and replace them with the bikini. No way would she allow him to do that, though. It was just way too...intimate.

"I'll go change in the stairwell," she said coldly, and turned her back on him so she could seek shelter in the relative safety of that enclosed space.

Once she was inside, she contemplated fleeing down the stairs so she wouldn't have to put the bathing suit on at all, but she refused to let him get to her that way. If he wanted to ogle her in a bikini, fine. It wouldn't be the first time she'd had to put herself on display.

Jaw set, she got out of her jeans and her top, folded them, and then removed her underwear and bra as well, tucking them between the other items of clothing so at least they wouldn't be sitting on top of the pile. It felt stranger than strange to be naked here in this industrial-looking stairwell with its steel diamond-plate stairs and gray-painted walls, and not much better even once she had the bikini on. But at least now she was partially covered...if only *very* partially. That bikini was even skimpier than it had looked before she put it on.

To help cover things up a bit, Bailey pulled the elastic band from the end of her braid and shook her hair loose, letting it fall over her shoulders. That was a little better. She hadn't paid much attention to her hair over the last six months, except to methodically braid it each day to keep it out of her way, but she could tell it had grown a lot, maybe because she'd basically left it alone. Now it fell more than halfway to her waist, the fine strands tickling her back below the bikini top's bottom band. Working quickly, she smoothed sunscreen onto her arms and legs and shoulders, and as much of her back as she could reach.

All right. She drew in a breath, squared her

shoulders, and went outside. The warm sunlight felt good on her bare skin, almost soothing—especially now that she didn't have to worry about getting a burn. Her gaze moved to where Nasim had been sitting on his lounger, but he wasn't there.

However, he hadn't gone very far. The pool's water rippled as he swam from side to side, his shoulder-length hair now sticking to the back of his neck. He didn't seem to be watching her or paying much attention to her movements, and she couldn't help but be relieved by that. At least this way she didn't feel quite so much as if she had to walk a gauntlet.

Moving quickly, she went to the edge of the pool and jumped in. The water was warm as well, much warmer than it should have been if it were only being heated by solar radiation. More djinn magic, she supposed. Nasim did seem to care a lot about making things comfortable.

Well, everything except the tension between them.

He surfaced and smiled when he saw her there, treading water. "Feels good, doesn't it?"

"Yes," she allowed. "Do you swim up here a lot?"

His grin broadened. "First time. I thought it shouldn't go to waste. It's probably been a long time since you got to swim in a pool, hasn't it?"

There was an understatement. Bailey had to consciously pause and thumb through her memories to recall the last time she'd gone swimming. It was…four years ago, she thought, when she and Diego were still together. One of his friends had a blow-out Memorial Day party at his house, and there had been a swimming pool. Even then, she hadn't really swum so much as sort of bobbed in the water with one arm around Diego and a margarita in her other hand.

"It's been a while," she allowed, then reached up with both hands to smooth her wet hair back from her face before paddling her way toward the shallow end so she could stand up. "What about you?"

"I can't recall exactly." Nasim swam over to the side of the pool and rested one arm on the concrete surround. "Probably longer than you. Air elementals aren't immediately drawn to water, but I have to say a swim can be refreshing."

"'Air elementals'?" Bailey echoed. "Is that what you are?"

"Yes." He paused and raised his face to the fresh breeze that blew across the rooftop patio. "We djinn come in four flavors—earth, air, fire, and water."

From the way he grinned at her as he spoke, she guessed he was teasing her a bit. Well, sorry if she didn't know there were different kinds of djinn. She'd spent too much time trying to elude them to stop and figure out if they differed from each other in any way.

"It would have been mainly air elementals who pursued you," Nasim went on. "While we can all blink from place to place, it's only those of us born to the air who can actually fly. That is why we make good scouts."

"Or reavers," Bailey said.

He frowned. "I told you I was not like them."

"Yeah, I got that part."

His expression cleared, and he swam over toward her, rising a bit from the water as his feet touched the bottom of the pool. This close, he was even more overwhelming, especially with water trickling its way over the impressive contours of his chest and stomach.

Bailey did her best to keep her eyes fixed on his face. Not that that part of him wasn't just as distracting.

"You need to relax," he said. A margarita glass appeared in each hand, and he extended one to her.

Relax, when she was trapped here with one of the djinn who'd helped to destroy the world? All right, the world itself wasn't exactly destroyed, but they'd sure done a good job of wiping out humanity.

But man, she was a sucker for a good margarita.

One hand reached out, almost of its own volition. Nasim allowed her to take hold of the margarita glass, but not before he let one of his fingers brush against hers. Briefly, a touch so quick that she almost didn't feel it at all.

But she did. One of those shivers trailed its way along her spine, despite the warmth of the sun beating down on them. For just a second, Bailey wondered exactly why she was going to all this work to have these races with Nasim, when it seemed clear enough to her that she would be all too willing to let their relationship become physical. Had she ever reacted to someone like this before? Usually, she was the ice queen, because it was just easier that way. Now, though…now she knew the heat awakening in her body didn't have much to do with the bright sun that shone down on them, or the almost blood-temperature water that buoyed her up now.

She took such a hasty swallow of her margarita that almost at once she got the dreaded "freezie" pain splitting through her temples. Goddamn it.

"Are you all right?" Nasim asked, after taking a more measured sip of his own drink.

"Fine," Bailey managed. "I just drank too fast."

"Ah."

The best way to beat a freezie was to have a bit more of what ailed you. She drank again, a small sip, one that slid much more easily down her throat. That was better.

"So," she said, "there are four kinds of djinn? Do you look different from each other? I mean, are all the fire elementals red-haired or something?"

Nasim's blue eyes crinkled with amusement. "No. You can't tell from looking at us what our natures are. Some fire elementals have flames appear around them if they are angry enough, but otherwise there really aren't any outward clues."

Well, Bailey supposed that was one way to tell whether someone was pissed off without having to ask them outright. The idea of a being who controlled fire was a little frightening to her, but that might only be because she was a native Californian, and so knew all too well how devastating fire could be when it got out of hand. Then again, after living through a couple of earthquakes, she wasn't sure whether an earth elemental would be much better. Air elementals seemed a bit less threatening, despite their role as scouts.

Or maybe that was just because the only djinn she knew was a spirit of the air.

Bailey sipped her margarita. The effects of that first gulp had now mostly disappeared, so she could enjoy her drink. It was very good, strong but not so strong that the tequila overwhelmed all the other ingredients.

Yeah, and strong enough that a couple of these could knock you on your ass if you aren't careful, she thought. *You get to have one. Just one.*

"But you can tell each other apart," she said.

"Yes, we can. It's something we djinn can sense about one another."

Like dogs, she thought, but didn't say anything out loud. She had a feeling that Nasim might not care for that particular comment. "Ah."

Another swallow, and then she went over to the side of the pool so she could set her margarita down. Since she was allowing herself only one, it seemed smarter to space out the sips from her drink. Once her hands were free, she swam out to the center of the pool and floated on her back, enjoying the warmth of the sun above and the water below.

Also, this way she had put some necessary distance between her and Nasim.

That didn't last for very long, though. She heard some faint splashes, and then he was there next to her, floating as well. Even though her eyes were mostly closed against the sun's glare, she thought she could still see the glimmer of water on his chest and stomach, sliding over the hard contours of his body.

"You seem more relaxed now."

"I am," she said. Well, mostly anyway. As long as she wasn't looking at him and thinking what it would be like to have those wet muscles pressed up against her...to have him reach for the ties to her bikini top and undo them, his hands cupping her breasts....

Shit. Some water or margarita or something seemed to get caught in the back of her throat, and Bailey coughed, losing her equilibrium and sinking down into the water. Nasim reached out and caught her by the arm before she could submerge completely.

"Are you all right?"

"Fine," she got out, and then coughed again. She sent him a rueful smile. "I think I should get out of the water for a while."

He wasn't floating now, either, but treading water a foot or so away from her. "Yes, maybe you should sit on one of the lounges."

It was hard to climb out of the pool, knowing he was watching her every step, but Bailey forced herself to go anyway, pausing to pick up her margarita from where she'd left it at the edge of the concrete near the deep end. As she walked toward the lounges, a bright towel patterned in blue and orange appeared on one of them, and she reached for it even as she put her drink down on one of the little tables that sat between the loungers.

Once the towel was wrapped around her, she felt a bit better. She was also glad to see that Nasim didn't seem inclined to follow her, but was now swimming the length of the pool, doing leisurely laps. Showing off, or just glad of the chance to get a bit of exercise?

Either way, he was giving her a little space, and she had to be glad of that. She dried herself off, then spread the towel on the chaise longue and leaned back. Once again, the margarita glass was in her hand, and she took another sip. Yes, that tasted good. Hard to believe that she could go through so many months of hunted living and somehow end up here on a rooftop deck, sipping a margarita and watching a particularly choice specimen of a man finally end his swim and pull himself up onto the edge of the pool, water dripping everywhere.

Not a man, though. He looked like one, but he wasn't.

Djinn…human…whatever. The view was still pretty damn nice, and she wasn't talking about L.A.'s skyline, hard and bright against the clear blue skies.

Nasim retrieved his own margarita and came to sit down next to her. He took a few swallows, then asked, "Looking forward to tomorrow?"

Bailey shifted on her lounge just enough so she could turn her head and give him a piercing look. "I haven't had enough to drink that I'm about to give away any of my secrets."

He put one hand to his chest in mock dismay. "I don't know why you would think such a thing of me."

"Because it's the kind of trick I would pull."

That remark elicited a chuckle. Nasim pushed his wet hair off his brow and stared across the rooftop toward the skyline she'd been observing just a moment earlier. "So you are the kind to play dirty."

"I didn't say that. There's a difference between taking advantage of a weakness and playing dirty."

"I see." He was silent for a moment, sipping at his margarita. "You like to win, don't you?"

Bailey shrugged. "Doesn't everyone?"

"It matters more to some people than to others."

"Let's just say I don't like to lose."

The amused expression left his face. He turned toward her, his gaze appraising. Not looking at her body, though, despite how much of it the bikini exposed. No, he was looking into her eyes, apparently trying to find some truth there. "Neither do I. But I promise you that when I win our bet, I'll be gracious."

"You mean when you lose and give me a first-class escort to Los Alamos."

He didn't blink. "As to that...in the unlikely

event that you do win, you may find that you don't enjoy it quite as much as you thought you would."

Bailey didn't reply…because she feared he just might be right.

SEVEN

Nasim made sure he was in the building's lobby at five minutes until noon, mainly because he wanted to be first on the scene. No real reason, except he thought it might put Bailey a bit off balance if he got there before she did. She'd departed the scene quickly enough the afternoon before, possibly because she hadn't wanted to respond to his remark about her reaction if she should manage to win their bet. He hadn't seen her after that, which didn't come as much of a surprise but disappointed him nonetheless. It would have been much better for the two of them to spend the evening together, to share some wine and food, even if nothing else came of it. Clearly, though, she seemed determined to keep as much distance between them as possible.

When she came out of the stairwell a few

minutes after he arrived in the lobby the next morning, she didn't seem all that surprised to see him. She gave him a nod and asked, "Ready?"

"Yes," he replied. "The cars are down in the garage."

"Lead on."

He took her to the stairs that led to the building's underground parking area, sending a little energy to the overhead lights so they wouldn't be descending into utter gloom. Although he didn't look back, Nasim could hear the sound of her boots echoing off the metal staircase. This morning she was completely covered from head to toe, in jeans and a T-shirt and the leather jacket she'd been wearing when he pulled her from the wreckage of her vehicle. He'd healed all the jacket's rips and scuffs, and had hoped she might comment on it. But it seemed today she was all business, focused on the contest ahead. While he was relieved to see her healthy and whole, he rather wished she wouldn't be quite so brisk, so independent.

The pair of Ferraris were parked not too far from the stairwell. Nasim extended a hand toward them. "The bluish-green one is yours."

Bailey lifted an ironic eyebrow. "You went with Ferraris?"

"Yes, I did," he replied, refusing to let her goad him. "They are excellent for a variety of driving conditions—*Motor Trend*'s 'Driver's Car of the Year,' you know."

This pronouncement made her chuckle out loud. "Where in the world did you see that?"

"I procured a number of periodicals from the central library to do my research."

"Oh, well, then." She went over to the blue-green sports car and looked it over. "Where did you get it?"

"From a dealership in Newport Beach. I already had mine, of course—that one came from Beverly Hills."

"Figures." Bailey glanced up from the Ferrari. "Did you just snap your fingers and make this one appear, too?"

"More or less. The key fob is already inside." No need to lock the vehicle or take any other measures to keep it safe—there was no one around to steal the car, no matter how valuable it might be.

"All right." She reached for the handle and lifted it. "Then let's get going, shall we?"

"Of course." Nasim went to his own vehicle and climbed in, touched his finger to the ignition. The engine roared to life, practically pulsing with power. Even though he controlled energies that most humans could barely comprehend, he had to admit that there was something primal about the rumble of the Ferrari's motor.

Something that made you want to race.

Bailey started up her own car and pulled slowly out of her parking space, heading for the ramp that led to street level. It seemed that she wanted to make sure he wouldn't have a difficult time following her, because she kept to the posted speed limits all the way to her destination, even though there was really no reason to drive so moderately. Still, she had to zig and zag a bit to get where she was going, and Nasim found himself glad that she wasn't speeding, since it would have been difficult to keep up.

To his surprise, she led him onto an on-ramp that emptied onto the freeway which cut through downtown. Once she was clear of the ramp, she moved into the second lane from the left and stopped. Nasim parked his vehicle next to hers and waited as she climbed out of the driver's seat and came over to him.

"This is a straight-up drag race," she told him, standing next to the window he'd obligingly rolled down. "The finish line is the junction with the 101 Freeway, about a mile and a half from here. Whoever gets to the overpass first wins—I set the cones out there so it'll be easy to tell where the race ends. Got it?"

"Yes," he replied, still a little startled that she would choose this type of race, especially in a car she'd never driven before. He didn't claim to be an expert, but at least he'd been behind the wheel of the Ferrari for a few days now, far more experience than Bailey had. Or at least, he guessed that someone with her background had never had the chance to drive something so expensive.

"Okay. We'll start when"—she leaned in toward him and squinted at the dashboard—"our clocks say it's ten minutes past noon. You jump the gun, you forfeit. Not a second sooner."

"I understand." Nasim could see why she'd had to come up with these makeshifts; it wasn't as though they had someone standing by with a flag or a starter pistol, and they certainly couldn't enlist any other djinn to offer their assistance.

"Good." With that, she sauntered back to her vehicle. Today she was all business in the leather jacket he'd repaired for her and with her hair pulled back into a severe braid, but she was still beautiful nonetheless.

Besides, he could remember what she'd looked like in that bikini.

But he couldn't allow himself to become distracted. He turned away from her and looked at the open freeway ahead of him. It was clear of vehicles, and the pavement looked smooth enough, even though no one had been around to maintain it for the past six months. This race would be straightforward, and would rely on brute speed and nothing else.

Although the day was warm, he turned off the vehicle's air conditioning. He didn't want to give up even a single ounce of horsepower for that kind of indulgence, because it would only slow him down.

His gaze moved to the digital clock on the dashboard. Nine minutes after twelve. Almost there. The car rumbled beneath him, obviously impatient with this prolonged idling. It wanted to be unleashed.

The digits on the clock changed. Twelve ten.

No stopping to think. His foot hit the accelerator, smashing it to the floorboard, and the Ferrari leapt forward like a startled horse. Beside him, Bailey's vehicle also surged forward, its nose even with his.

Damn.

The accelerator was already floored, but he shifted into second and rapidly into third, seeing that he was already going eighty miles an hour. Ninety. One hundred. Outside the windows, concrete pillars holding up overpasses flashed past in a blur, but he couldn't let himself be distracted.

Shifting into fourth, blazing past a hundred and ten miles per hour.

And Bailey's bluish Ferrari was ahead by a nose.

How was that possible? Perhaps she knew some arcane form of speed shifting that had given her an advantage. Or perhaps her car was just slightly newer, just slightly more powerful.

Nasim's hands clenched on the steering wheel as he kept the accelerator pressed toward the floor. And yet she inched ahead again, not by much, but certainly enough to make the distance between them feel like a light-year.

The overpass was coming up. He could see it, had to ignore all the lanes veering off to the right so they might connect with the other freeway, the one whose overpass would mark the endpoint of the race. Now they were down to three lanes—not that it mattered, since there was no one to share the roadway with them.

"Come on, come on," he muttered, even though the Ferrari really couldn't do much more than it already was. They had left 120 miles per hour in the dust a few yards back, and still the speedometer was steadily moving over to the right.

It didn't matter, though, because in the next second, Bailey's car had shot under the overpass, with Nasim trailing her by almost a foot. As soon as she was clear of the overpass, she slowed down, coming to a stop near an exit that proclaimed it led into Chinatown. He slowed as well, his nerve endings still thrumming with adrenaline. How had she managed it? Identical vehicles with no modifications. No reason at all for him to have lost...except that she was the better driver.

He put the Ferrari in park, then got out. Bailey also climbed out of her vehicle, smiling.

Of course she was smiling. She'd just beaten him.

"Congratulations," he said, extending a hand. Although he was disappointed and annoyed with himself, he certainly didn't want her to see that he was a bad sport.

"Thanks," she replied. At least she did take his hand and shake it. Her fingers were warm, stronger than he'd imagined they would be. "The Ferraris were a good choice," she added as she pulled her hand from his—but gently, in a way that seemed to signal she was doing so because it would be rather silly to keep on shaking hands once they'd made the initial gesture.

"I'm glad you think so." He glanced at the off-ramp, the one with the sign that directed those exiting there toward Chinatown. "Can I buy you lunch?"

Was this a date? She didn't think so. It was only lunch, and Nasim had been joking about "buying" her their midday meal, since of course no one was left to charge for food.

Still, it was sort of surreal to sit here in a booth in one of Chinatown's kitschiest restaurants, with darkly flocked wallpaper that looked like it had been there since the 1970s, and tanks still full of fish floating around aimlessly, highlighted by strategically placed colored lights. How those fish were still alive, Bailey had no idea. After six months of neglect, of no fresh water and no food, they should have all been little desiccated corpses lying on the Day-Glo sand at the bottom of their tanks. But there they were.

It didn't make much sense. Then again, there was a whole lot about this new world that didn't make any sense.

Nasim had taken her to a booth tucked away in the back of the restaurant. She wondered if he'd brought her to this shadowy spot so he could make a move on her, but so far he'd been acting like a perfect gentleman, asking her what her favorite dishes were, what kind of drink she liked best. Even Diego had never been so solicitous, and Bailey wasn't sure how she was supposed to react. Probably best to pretend this was all perfectly normal, even if it was anything but. She sipped a mai tai complete with paper umbrella, and wondered just how she'd gotten here.

A wave of Nasim's hand, and the table was filled with a variety of dishes—chicken fried rice, egg drop soup, sweet and sour chicken, a plate of dim sum. The mingled aromas were enough to set Bailey's mouth watering. Yes, the lo mein she'd found in the fridge in her borrowed loft had been pretty decent, but it had lost a little something from being reheated. All of the food before her was piping hot and, she guessed, probably of higher quality than what this restaurant had actually served back in the day.

Nasim dished a little bit of everything for her, then filled his own plate. She raised her glass, and he clinked his own—a daiquiri, not a mai tai—against hers.

"Thanks for the feast," she said.

"I'm glad I could provide it," he replied. "The location suggested itself, after all."

Bailey supposed it had. "You're a very gracious loser."

The smile he'd been wearing didn't fade. "Ah, well, I have another day to redeem myself."

True enough. That was the entire reason why she'd gone for the whole "best two out of three" plan, although now she was kicking herself for suggesting it in the first place. If they'd done a "winner take all" setup, she would already be free and on the road to Los Alamos.

For some reason, though, that prospect didn't seem quite as appealing as she'd thought it would be.

Besides, all this was predicated on a pretty big

if—whether Nasim would even honor the bet they'd made. So far he hadn't given any sign that he wouldn't, but Bailey knew she was fooling herself if she didn't acknowledge that he was the one who held all the cards here. She could drive like the wind, but he was a djinn, and she was only human. It wasn't much of a contest, once you got down to the basics. However, she wouldn't let herself dwell on the inequities that existed between them. Maybe she was being naïve, but she wanted to believe that he wouldn't pull out of their bet if things didn't go his way.

"Any ideas on tomorrow's race?" she inquired after taking a sip of her mai tai.

"No," he said, and something about the slightly perplexed expression he wore told her that he was probably being truthful.

"Well, you have the rest of today and tomorrow morning to figure it out." She reached with her chopsticks and snagged a piece of dim sum, then took a bite.

"You would like to keep our little races set for high noon?"

"Why not? It's a good time of day, because with the sun directly overhead, you don't have to worry about dealing with any glare coming in through the windshield."

Nasim nodded. "I suppose I should have thought of that. You're right, of course. Well, then, yes, I suppose I have nearly a day to decide what kind of race we'll have, and where."

"And what about the cars?" Bailey asked. She sipped her mai tai again. "It's my turn to choose, but I can't exactly snap my fingers and make them appear the way you can."

"You'll have to tell me," he replied. He also used chopsticks—quite expertly—to guide a mouthful of chicken fried rice to his lips. "I suppose if you make your decision by ten or so in the morning, I'll have enough time to locate the cars in question."

He sounded completely confident, and Bailey supposed he was. After all, she hadn't been exaggerating about the finger snapping—that seemed to be just about all he had to do to get whatever she wanted. Maybe if she went really crazy and requested a pair of numbers-matching '63 split-window Corvettes, it might take him a little more effort than simply locating a couple of abandoned Ferraris left behind on car lots here in Southern California, but she had no doubt that he could eventually pull it off. Not that she would ask for something so esoteric, mostly because, while classic cars could be fun to drive, they couldn't match the performance of their modern counterparts.

"I will," she said. "How about I slip a note under your door?"

That suggestion got her a slightly pained glance, but Nasim only shrugged. "If that's how you want to manage things."

"Why not? It adds a little mystery to the process."

He chuckled. "If you say so."

They ate quietly for a moment. The food was wonderful, and so completely different from anything she'd had during the six months—or really, a lot longer than that, since she hadn't eaten Chinese for a while even before the Heat came along—that she wanted to pay attention to it, savor every individual flavor.

"How did you know to conjure such great Chinese food?"

"It's not a matter of conjuring," Nasim replied, "but only remembering. Once I've eaten a dish, I can recall what it tasted like and re-create it. I suppose it's a talent all we djinn possess."

"Handy," Bailey remarked, "considering I can't even boil water."

"What's so difficult about boiling water?" he inquired, brows pulling together. "It only needs to reach a certain temperature."

She shrugged. "I suppose it's just an expression that means I can't cook. Like, at all. It's microwaves and takeout for me—well, back when those things still existed, I mean."

Something about Nasim's expression looked

almost guilty, although Bailey wondered if that was just a trick of the restaurant's dim lighting. Or maybe he did feel some kind of remorse for what his people had done to the world, even if he hadn't been directly involved. It was too personal a question to ask, so she put it aside for now. She didn't want to get personal. She wanted to talk about the logistics of their races, or maybe something innocuous like the food they were eating, and that was about it.

Because the truth was, even though Nasim had seated himself a decorous enough distance from her, she was still far too aware of his presence. Today he was back in his black T-shirt and jeans, but she remembered what he'd looked like the day before in his swim trunks, how the water had slid lovingly over those gorgeous muscles of his, how the sun had picked out golden lights in his sandy hair.

Mentally, she might be racing to get away from him, but her body apparently had other ideas. Damn it, she didn't have time for this kind of crap.

"No one ever taught me," she said quickly, wrenching her thoughts away from Nasim's physical perfection. "To cook, I mean."

"Because you were in foster homes."

"Yes." Bailey reached for her mai tai and took a large swallow, one that almost drained the glass.

No big deal, obviously, because in the next second, it was refilled to within half an inch of the rim. She arched an eyebrow at Nasim. "Are you trying to get me drunk? It's going to take more than a couple of mai tais, especially with all this food."

"I'll remember that." A small smile played around the corners of his lips. "But no, I was merely trying to make sure that you had enough to drink with the food that's remaining."

"You could always just get me some water."

"Where's the fun in that?"

It was her turn to shake her head. She picked up a few pieces of sweet and sour chicken and ate them slowly, savoring the tangy blend of flavors.

"You don't like to talk about it, do you?" Nasim inquired.

"About what?"

"Being in a foster family."

The chicken seemed to stick in her throat. Bailey picked up her drink and took another swallow, a little smaller than the one from a moment earlier. Of course, Nasim was right; she didn't like to talk about it. If she could have had her way, she would have erased that part of her life permanently from her memory. Unfortunately, it didn't work that way. She remembered far too much.

She set down her glass. "What do you want to know? How I got bounced around from house to house until I was ten, finally got someplace that seemed stable, only to have one of my foster mothers get breast cancer a few years later? How the house they sent me to after that seemed great on the surface—foster father was a judge, foster mother was a teacher—except that foster daddy liked to diddle pubescent girls, and that's why they took in foster kids?"

Nasim was silent, staring at her. "I am sorry. I had no idea—"

"Oh, don't worry," Bailey cut in. "I was little young for his taste when I first went to live there, but I figured out his game soon enough. Two days after my thirteenth birthday, he tried to come into my bedroom, but I'd gotten a knife from one of the boys at school and stuck it in the judge's fat gut. Didn't kill him, but it sure made him think twice about trying to put his dick in me. Of course, they hushed the whole thing up, because the judge couldn't lose his position, right? I got off easy—instead of juvie, they sent me to a group home. It wasn't so bad there, because word had gotten around about what I'd done and everyone pretty much left me alone. I moved out when I was eighteen because I got a monthly check from the county if I stayed in school and worked. And that's my life in a nutshell. Satisfied?"

Of course, she'd left out how she'd met Oscar at the car show, had gone to work with him—had fallen in love with his son. But as much as Oscar appreciated her skills with engines, he didn't think she was good enough for Diego. Once Oscar found out about his son's relationship with the girl he'd taken under his wing, that was the end of the story. She was out of a job and a boyfriend, and apparently Diego hadn't been so in love with her that he wanted to risk his future in his father's business. Bailey was on her own…again.

Luckily, she'd always been pretty good at taking care of herself.

Nasim didn't immediately answer her question. He stared at her, his gaze troubled, as though he wasn't sure how to choose the correct response.

No big deal. Bailey honestly wasn't sure whether there was one. She picked up her chopsticks, fumbling with them a little because having to recite all that crap to a djinn, of all people, had rattled her more than she wanted to admit. Staring down at her plate, she said, her tone fierce, "Don't you dare feel sorry for me."

"I don't feel sorry for you," Nasim said softly. "I admire you."

She hadn't been expecting that response. Gaze still fixed on her food, she said, "What's to admire? I did what I had to do to survive, just like I've been doing ever since you djinn changed the world." Abruptly, she set down her chopsticks and pushed her plate away. "I think I'm full."

A frown pulled at Nasim's brows, but he looked more troubled than mad at her for bailing out on him. "Bailey, I didn't mean to upset you."

"I'm not upset," she said. It was a lie, of course, but she had to hope he wouldn't argue with her about it. "I've eaten enough. The food's really rich. I'm going to go back to my loft."

Before he could say anything, make some kind of attempt to get her to stay, she pushed her way out of the booth and stood up. Luckily, the key fob for the Ferrari was in her pocket, so she could just leave on her own. Well, unless Nasim used a little of his djinn magic to make the key disappear...or maybe the car itself.

If he did, then she'd just walk back. She'd walked much farther than that when she'd left the group at Caltech and had come to hide here in downtown L.A.

But apparently he guessed that she was way too on edge, and that any interference on his part would only anger her that much more. Looking sad rather than angry, he said, "Of course. I'll be along once I've finished my food."

Which was his way of saying that he was allowing her enough space to leave and get her head together. Funny how a djinn seemed to be better at dealing with her than most—well, all—of the human men she'd known.

"Okay," she replied, then marched out of the

restaurant. It had been so dim inside that the bright sunlight which greeted her made her blink and pull the sunglasses out of her jacket pocket. She was glad of them, glad of the way they hid her eyes.

Los Angeles might have been a ghost town, but she still didn't want the world to see the way she began to sob as she hurried over to the Ferrari and peeled out of the parking lot.

EIGHT

Bailey's steel-blue Ferrari was parked on the street behind her Porsche when Nasim returned to his loft. Not so surprising, he supposed; she didn't have a key card to the building's underground parking garage, and he'd closed the gates behind him as he left. He wasn't even sure why exactly, except that they had been closed when he first came to dwell here, and he thought it better to maintain the illusion that the place was unoccupied. Foolish in a way, since anyone watching would have seen the two sports cars drive away earlier this morning, might have noticed the two of them swimming in the rooftop pool, or seen her car parked where it hadn't been a few days earlier.

That thought made him blink himself back to the roof, just to satisfy himself that there was no one around to observe anything he and Bailey were up to. The skies remained clear, and he could see all the way to the Pacific Ocean, a thin blue line at the extreme western edge of his line of sight. Somewhere between here and there was the community of djinn and Chosen in Bel-Air, but certainly none of them had ventured anywhere near the heart of Los Angeles.

Downtown was still his...and Bailey's.

He thought of what she had said during their lunch, of all the tragedies in her life, tragedies she'd done her best to underplay by describing those events in a hard, flat tone, as though they'd happened to someone else. No wonder she'd done such a good job of keeping herself safe all these months. She'd been doing much the same thing for her entire life. The world might have changed, but her instinct for survival hadn't.

More than anything, he wanted to go down to her loft, knock on the door, and tell her that he understood her suffering and did not think less of her for the hardships she'd endured. No, he admired her even more now, an admiration still mixed with desire. He wanted her, true, but more than that, he wanted to prove that he was worthy of her. Being the victor in this contest they'd concocted was more important than ever, but more because he wanted her to admire him, to see that they could work together as equals despite his being a djinn and her being human. Before he'd met her, he certainly would not have considered a human his equal, no matter what qualities they might have possessed. Now he saw that he had, quite simply, been wrong.

However, Nasim knew she needed this time alone. Opening up to him had been difficult for her, and he sensed that intruding now would only make her shut down again. Better to let it go for the moment and hope for better things in the future.

Besides, he needed to figure out what tomorrow's course would be.

He went back down to his loft and stood at the window, surveying L.A.'s skyline. Not to admire it this time, but to determine what sort of challenge he could present Bailey with, one that would allow her to acquit herself well but would still give him the opportunity to emerge the victor.

They'd already had a straight-out drag race, so it seemed they should do some street racing this time instead. This was a calculated risk, just because he'd seen her drive and knew she excelled at navigating her way through the streets of downtown.

Fine, then…they would race somewhere else. Nasim knew he could transport them basically anywhere in the area, so the venue wasn't a problem. Someplace where the terrain would present a challenge, although he knew he couldn't do anything as extreme as sending them to race out in the desert. While the idea had merit, it would only work if they drove specialized vehicles, and with Bailey making the choice, that meant she would most likely come up with something which wouldn't be suitable for racing in sand.

His gaze moved past the high-rises of downtown to the hills beyond. He'd spent enough time in the area that he knew several roads went up and over the Hollywood Hills, twisting their way along narrow, scenic routes that once carried far more traffic than they were originally designed for. Now, of course, there was no one left to drive on them.

That didn't mean they were empty, however. He would have to go and scout the route, make sure any vehicles abandoned there as their drivers succumbed to the Heat were pushed safely off to the side of the road or removed altogether, depending on how much of an obstruction they created.

Before he had even decided on this loft as his home base, he had summoned a map of the greater Los Angeles area to him, knowing he would need to utilize it to get around efficiently. He spread it out on the dining room table now, eyes scanning the twisted mass of streets that had once been one of the world's most populated areas. Yes, there were the hills he had thought would present something of a driving challenge, and there was the street that twisted along at almost the crown of those hills.

Mulholland Drive.

It stretched a long ways, probably farther than they really needed to drive during this particular contest. His finger traced the route as it looped back and forth. Yes, there was a good start and end point. Now he just had to go take a look for himself.

The blink of an eye, and he stood in the middle of the road, surveying his surroundings. Off to his left was a gate that led into what was no doubt a multimillion-dollar mansion. To his right was an open expanse of some scrubby dry grass, and an exit lane leading onto Coldwater Canyon Boulevard.

And ahead of him was a distressing number of abandoned vehicles. He could already tell that the road was too narrow for him to simply push them up against the curb, which meant he would have to send those cars he couldn't divert into driveways somewhere else entirely. Even for a djinn, that sort of endeavor would require a good deal of effort—and time.

Then again, with Bailey retreated into her loft

for the rest of the day, what else did he have but time?

One sweep first, to relocate whichever cars he could onto driveways and side streets. It surprised him that there had been so many vehicles out and about when the Heat descended, for he'd thought that people would have done their best to remain at home while such a deadly disease was ravaging the city. Then again, it seemed to him that very few of those who'd lived here in Los Angeles had dwelled anywhere near their place of business, and so it was most likely that they'd been attempting to return home from work when they succumbed to the fever.

The thought saddened him. At the outset of this endeavor, he'd been largely indifferent to the fate of humanity. They had been given this world and done their best to destroy it, and so he hadn't thought he would shed many tears over their loss. None of them had been individuals, only a faceless mass that needed to be swept away so the djinn could take control.

Now, though…now he looked at these abandoned vehicles, and he thought of those who had been driving them, desperate to reach home before the fever overtook them completely, bewildered by the strange doom that had descended upon them all. No one had known what was happening to them. It must have seemed like an act of God, a cruel fate given out to those who thought they could not be deserving of such calamity.

God had very little to do with it, though. Nasim supposed He could have intervened, if He had been so inclined, but none of the djinn had seen any sign of such intervention. No, they had been allowed to carry out their plan, and it had been more successful than even its masterminds had hoped.

Those masterminds, however, probably had not stopped to think about how messy the aftermath would be. The disease killed cleanly—they'd made sure of that—but it had still left behind all these relics of mankind's existence here on earth—cars and trucks and trains and planes and high-rises and factories and everything else. Some could be retained, but the vast majority, such as the vehicles strewn on Mulholland Drive, would have to be disposed of one way or another.

Just as he was doing now.

The first sweep completed, he went back the way he had come, laying a hand on a car hood here, or on the bed of a truck there. As he did so, he imagined them all being transported to the parking lot at the Hollywood Bowl, the closest venue he could think of to accommodate so many vehicles at once.

By the time he was done, the sun had already

begun to drop behind the westernmost spur of these hills, although it would be some time before it set completely. A djinn could not become physically tired the way a human might, and yet Nasim could still tell that his efforts had sapped him somewhat. Nothing that a good night's sleep and some food couldn't repair, of course. Even so, he had to wonder a little at himself, that he would go to so much work for a confrontation that would last only ten minutes or so at the most, especially since this was the sort of driving Bailey tended to excel at.

Well, he would just have to see how she did the next day.

It was with something of a feeling of accomplishment that he blinked himself back to his loft. He waved a hand to turn on one of the table lamps in the living room area and headed toward the kitchen, intent on a nice bottle of Viognier he'd left chilling in the fridge.

He'd only just removed the cork when he heard a somewhat diffident knock at the door. Surprised, he went over to answer that knock and saw Bailey standing out in the hallway, her expression a curious mix of hesitancy and bravado.

"I picked the cars for tomorrow," she said, and thrust a piece of paper at him. "I tried knocking earlier, but—"

"I was out setting up the course for our race,"

he replied, taking the piece of paper she offered before stuffing it into one of the pockets in his jeans. "Why don't you come in? I've just opened a bottle of wine."

Her gaze moved past him to the Viognier where it sat on the kitchen counter. "I'm not sure—"

"We're driving tomorrow, not this evening," he said. "A glass or two isn't going to hurt anything."

One corner of her mouth lifted slightly. "I learned drinking from the best of the best. Of course a glass of wine isn't going to do much."

"Then come in."

Another hesitation, and then he saw her shoulders lift slightly, as if she knew that declining his offer would make it seem as though she was not quite as sure of herself as she pretended to be. "Okay."

Nasim stepped aside and she came in, moving toward the kitchen. "You were getting the course set up, huh? It must not be anywhere around here."

Of course she was correct, but he still asked, "What makes you say that?"

Once again her mouth quirked. "Because I was spying on you."

"Spying?" He went around the bar and got some glasses from the cupboard, then poured a measure of white wine for both of them. "How so?"

"After I knocked on your door, I went up to the roof and looked around. I figured if you weren't here, you must be out somewhere getting ready for tomorrow. I didn't see any sign of you, though."

He handed her a glass of wine and said, "No, it isn't anywhere around here. But that's the only hint I'm going to give you." Now that he had one hand free, he reached in his pocket and drew out the slightly crumpled piece of paper she'd given him. "Nissan GT-R," he read out loud. Nasim would be the first to admit that he wasn't precisely a connoisseur of high-end automobiles, but he was rather surprised to read that car manufacturer's name rather than a host of other contenders.

Bailey must have sensed his skepticism, because she lifted an eyebrow at him before she raised the glass of wine to her lips and took a sip. "Don't act so surprised. The GT-R is a serious performer. You'll see."

"I suppose I shall," he replied, unperturbed. He had no reason to doubt her choice, and he hoped that, because it was a Nissan, it wouldn't be terribly difficult to procure.

She nodded, then moved past him to stand by the window. The glass and steel towers of downtown L.A. were warmed by the light of the setting sun, gleaming like golden spires. The warm light caught in Bailey's fair hair, turning it nearly gold as well. Without looking at him, she said, "I'm sorry about before."

"'Sorry'?" he echoed, not sure what she meant.

"My little nervous breakdown at lunch."

"Ah." Nasim came closer but made sure not to get too close. At times she reminded him of a wary wild animal, easily spooked and ready to bolt at the slightest abrupt movement. "I would hardly call that a nervous breakdown. Actually, I should be thanking you for your honesty."

Bailey didn't seem mollified by that remark. "I figured you might as well know the truth," she said, then sipped at her wine again. "I mean, I never did much to hide my upbringing. What would be the point? But that other thing…I didn't talk about that."

He didn't have to ask what she meant by "that other thing." It was certainly nothing to be ashamed of—she'd only been defending herself—but he could see why bringing it up would be difficult, especially since the man in question had been someone with some social standing, a person who could have made her life even harder than it already was if he determined that she hadn't protected his secret after all. "You never told anyone?"

"No. Not even Diego."

"Who was Diego?" Nasim asked, hoping he didn't sound like a jealous lover. Truth be told, he had experienced a twinge of envy at the sound of the strange man's name on Bailey's lips, even though this Diego had to have died along with almost everyone else when the Heat took over the world.

A lift of her shoulders, one that seemed a little too practiced. "He was my boyfriend for a while. He knew a lot about cars. But I didn't bother to say anything to him because I knew it would only make him angry. I wasn't going to get revenge for myself, but he might have. Not that he was a violent person or anything, but he grew up in a rough part of town. He knew people who knew people, if you know what I mean. The last thing I needed was that fat bastard shot in the head as he was driving home from the grocery store, because with my luck, the cops would've tried to pin it on me. Anyway"—she let out a breath and drank some more wine—"it wasn't worth the risk."

No, he supposed not. All the same, Nasim halfway wished the Heat hadn't been quite as fatal as it proved to be. That way, Bailey's attacker might have lived...and Nasim could have hunted him down and cut out his black heart.

"I can see that," he said, his tone neutral. Then he added, in an attempt to lighten the conversation, "What happened to slipping the note under the door?"

She looked at him blankly for a moment, then smiled. A small smile, but one that Nasim was glad to see nonetheless. "I didn't know how long it would take you to track down the cars, so I figured I might as well give you as much time as possible."

"Well, thank you for that. It's not so difficult to locate them most of the time. If we were out in the middle of Nebraska, I suppose it would be more trouble, but here in Los Angeles, everything seems to be within easy reach."

His comment made her smile widen a little, and he was glad to see it. "I hadn't thought of it that way, but you're probably right. So you'll just snap your fingers tomorrow morning, and we'll drive off to wherever you want us to race?"

"Yes." Driven by a sudden impulse, he said, "Are you hungry? It's been many hours since our lunch."

All of a sudden she was wary again, body tense, smile gone. "Not really. That was a big meal."

"Of which you ate very little." She didn't respond right away, and he went on, "I can get you anything you like. Please, stay and eat with me. It seems foolish for us to be taking such solitary meals when we're staying right next to one another."

A long pause, during which he waited without drawing breath, without doing anything that might make her demur. Then at last she pushed her braid back over her shoulder and replied, "I suppose you're right. But don't blame me if I try to pick your brain and get some clues about our race tomorrow."

He smiled at her, relieved that she hadn't continued to resist the notion of them sharing a meal. "You are certainly welcome to try."

———

This probably was a stupid idea, but once she'd agreed to stay and eat, Bailey knew she had to keep her promise to Nasim. He'd asked her what she'd like for dinner, and she told him he might as well come up with something that would go with the white wine they were already drinking. No way was she going to let him trick her into sharing a second bottle. She could hold her liquor with the best of them, but she knew that having more than a few glasses might start to impair her judgment, let alone affect her performance the next day.

No matter what Nasim had up his sleeve, she was determined to beat him two times in a row.

For now, though, she had to sit here and pretend that she wasn't staring at the way the sleeves of his black T-shirt strained against his biceps, or noticing how the dim lighting in the loft only seemed to emphasize his strong cheekbones and the sensual, ironic curve of his mouth. Really, she needed to get it together. Since when had some eye candy ever managed to put her off her stride?

They were eating linguine with pesto sauce, something light yet still rich with olive oil and basil. Salads, too, and bread as well. Way more carbs than she would have eaten in the bad old days, when she never knew if she'd have to drag out the old bikini or short-shorts to play spokesmodel at a car show, but after so many months of privation, she figured a bit of carb loading probably couldn't do too much harm.

He hadn't said anything more about that pervy old goat of a judge who'd tried to rape her. However, Nasim still seemed interested in her past, although at least this time he'd moved on to the more neutral topic of her obsession with cars.

"Who taught you to drive?" he asked.

"Maura," she replied, then added, "One of my foster mothers. They were lesbians." *Might as well get that out in the open right away,* Bailey thought.

Nasim didn't seem too fazed. "Women who

love other women. We djinn have them as well, and also men who prefer the company of men."

Well, that was an interesting tidbit. She didn't know why she'd kept thinking of the djinn as one big, monolithic block of heterosexual men, when clearly they had to have both sexes. It was probably because she'd only seen male djinn giving pursuit, not any of their women. Apparently the females of their race weren't as bloodthirsty as the men, or at least they had better things to do with their time than hunt down a bunch of helpless humans.

"Got it," she said. "I told you how one of my foster mothers got breast cancer, right?"

Nasim nodded.

"For a while, Maura and Terri—she was the one who had cancer—really tried to keep it together, tried to keep their foster kids. But Maura was overwhelmed, naturally, and even though I was just a kid, she taught me to drive so I could go to the corner store and get a few things for the house if necessary."

"No one noticed?" he asked, clearly surprised.

"No," Bailey replied. At the time, she was sure she was going to get in all kinds of trouble. But she'd been tall for her age, and developed early, and if she put on some sunglasses and some lip gloss and acted like she knew what she was doing, no one asked any questions. "And it made it easier later on, when I was in the group home, because I passed my driving test on the first try, even though I didn't have anyone to teach me when I was supposedly the right age."

Nasim lifted a forkful of linguine to his lips and chewed thoughtfully. "Many people drive, but it isn't their passion. Why did it become yours?"

"Because…." She stopped there, not sure she wanted to tell him how she felt when behind the wheel, as though she was finally free and could go anywhere and do anything. That wasn't precisely true, but the perception still lingered despite everything. "Well, at the group home, someone had left behind a ton of car magazines—*Motor Trend, Car and Driver, Hot Rod, Car Craft.* I read them all, and when I turned sixteen and could get a job, I always used some of my money to buy new magazines. Yeah, they were all online, but there was something about holding the magazine in my hands, being able to go back and read things over and over. Anyway, that's why. And then Oscar gave me a chance to work in his shop, to actually wrench on cars and drive them, and I learned even more. So here we are."

Bailey reached for her glass of wine and took a large swallow, thinking she'd said enough. Her djinn companion was watching her with both speculation and compassion in his gaze, and she wasn't sure what to make of that. Had he been able to read between the lines of what she'd said, to guess that she used cars as a way to escape, to pretend the world didn't suck quite as much as it actually did? It was hard to tell, and she sure as hell couldn't ask him.

"It's quite an accomplishment, considering," he said.

"Considering what?" she flared. "That I came from such a shitty background?"

"No," he said mildly. "For someone as young as you."

"I'm not that young. I'm twenty-four."

He only smiled, and Bailey realized what a ridiculous statement that had been. How old was Nasim? He didn't look that much older than she, but djinn were basically immortal, weren't they? That was the impression she'd gotten from the few things the scientist in Los Alamos had said, although she'd been focused on more important matters, such as how to kill them, or at least how to evade them. It certainly wasn't that she'd read about them in storybooks or anything like that; her childhood had been noticeably short on whimsy.

To cover up her embarrassment, she said, "You practice at anything enough, you get good at it. And I've had a lot of practice these last seven months."

The smile faded. "Yes, I suppose you have."

Her remark had hit a nerve, she could tell. Well, it wasn't as if he hadn't participated in those chases, although she still hadn't been able to figure out exactly why he'd decided to pursue her in the first place. His intent clearly hadn't been the same as that of the other djinn who'd hunted her all over downtown. Was he really just looking to have a fling with a human? There had to have been easier ways to go about it than wasting time on car chases.

Or maybe not. Nasim's fellow djinn had been ruthless when it came to eliminating human survivors. It was entirely possible that she was the only mortal female in a hundred-mile radius.

Bailey didn't want to think about that, though. Her childhood had made her pretty good at compartmentalizing things, so she'd done her best to forget about the people she'd hunkered down with for a time, gorgeous would-be actress Leila and super-competent Tyrell and all the rest of them. They had to be dead after so many months. There was absolutely no way they could have survived this long.

"Anyway," she said, "what about you? For a djinn, you seem to know your way around a car."

"'For a djinn'?" he echoed, that amused quirk returning to his mouth.

"Well, seeing how you can just pop in and out of existence whenever you choose—or fly through the air—it doesn't seem as though you really need to bother with driving cars."

"True," he admitted, fingers playing with the stem of his wine glass. "Although not all of us can fly, just the air elementals."

"Still."

"You're correct about driving. Some of us learned, just because we found it amusing, but I had no experience until a few days ago. I realized that the only way to catch up with you was to teach myself to drive...so I did."

For a moment, all Bailey could do was stare at Nasim as he swallowed some more wine, then returned to his linguine. Was he serious? Had he really just learned to drive a couple of days ago? It was no small blow to her pride to realize this man —this djinn—had become almost as good a driver as she was in so short an amount of time. Where was the fairness in that?

Well, she'd learned a long time ago that life sure as hell wasn't fair. Nasim's almost instant prowess behind the wheel was just more evidence of that fundamental truth. Besides, he was a djinn. The same rules didn't apply to him.

"Congratulations," she said dryly. "It takes most people years to drive like you do."

"You're angry."

He'd made the statement in a calm tone, with nothing of accusation in it, but Bailey could feel herself bristling all the same. "No, I'm not," she replied. "Irritated, maybe."

"Isn't that almost the same thing?"

It was her turn to smile. "Believe me, Nasim…you'll know when I'm angry."

He chuckled. "I suppose I will."

Nothing seemed to faze him. Bailey supposed that must be because he knew he had the upper hand here. She had to accept the situation, since there wasn't much she could do to change it.

Except win tomorrow, of course. If she beat him a second time in a row, they would be done.

To change the subject, she said, "You're sure you'll be able to get the cars?"

"I already told you I would. These are late-model vehicles, and Los Angeles was a city that loved its cars. It will not be a problem."

No, it seemed there wasn't any situation he encountered that he couldn't handle…which annoyed the hell out of her.

"Well," she said, setting her napkin down on the tabletop and pushing her chair back, "I should probably go. We have a big day tomorrow, and I want to be rested for it."

His brow creased slightly, but she noticed the way his gaze slid to her plate, which was now empty, and to the wine glass that sat next to that plate and which was also empty. This wasn't like lunch, when she'd bolted before she was even halfway finished with her food. There was no real reason for her to remain here any longer.

"Of course," he said, his tone formal. He also set his napkin aside and stood up. "I'm glad you stayed for dinner."

"It was great. Thank you." Which was only the truth, but the words still sounded forced. There wasn't much she could do about it, though, so she got up from her chair and began to make her way to the front door.

Nasim followed her. Just as she was about to put her hand on the knob, he spoke.

"You want very badly to win, don't you?"

Slowly, she turned around to face him. He stood a foot or so away, arms at his side, his expression showing only a sort of pleasant curiosity. "Yes," she replied, glad that the single syllable sounded firm enough, even though deep down, she knew she wasn't quite as certain about the situation as she wanted to be.

"Is that because you really do want to get away from me, or because you just hate to lose?"

"I—" Why was she hesitating? She did want to get away from him, away from here. She wanted to be someplace where she knew the djinn could never hurt her. Not that she was worried about Nasim hurting her, but....

He stepped closer. "Which is it, Bailey?"

Why wouldn't the words come out? She stared

up at him and realized he was very near now, so close she could smell the scent of pine and dry, sun-warmed grass in his hair or maybe his clothes, as though he'd spent all afternoon outdoors some-place where he'd be near those kinds of trees and plants.

Her feet felt as if they'd been nailed to the floor. She knew she should move away, should reach out and turn the doorknob and hurry back to her own loft, and yet she remained there, immobile, as if he'd cast some kind of spell on her.

"Ah," he said, and then his hands were cupping her face, his touch tender, far more gentle than she'd expected, holding her as if she was some sort of fragile soap bubble he feared might break.

When his lips touched hers, she was shocked by the heat that flooded through her, the need, the desire, the ache between her legs that told her she wanted this, wanted it so badly that she would have been fine with him tearing her clothes off then and there, fine with him carrying her over to the couch so they could consummate the tension that had been growing between them the past few days.

Somehow, though, she retained enough control to pull herself away. "No," she said, and again, "*No.*"

And she opened the door and fled.

NINE

Nasim knew better than to pursue her. It had been a risk to even steal that kiss, but her hesitation had spoken volumes—and so had the way she'd stood there, wary but with her lips slightly parted, a warm glow in her blue eyes telling him that she was not quite so standoffish as she wanted to appear. And he had felt how she'd responded…before reason kicked in and she took herself away from the situation before anything else could happen.

Although he had wanted another kiss—and more—it was better to leave matters where they stood for now. She needed time to decide what it was she truly wanted. He supposed he would find out the next day, for if she drove like the devil himself was after her, then he would know she desired her freedom more than she desired him.

In the meantime, he located two of the vehicles she'd requested, one at a dealership in Santa Monica, and the other farther south, in Huntington Beach. They now waited down in the garage for their trial the next morning. In fact, it was beginning to look like the world's most expensive used car lot down there, what with Bailey's Porsche—which he'd moved off the street —the pair of Ferraris, and now the two Nissan super-cars.

The image made him smile slightly. His body ached for Bailey, true, but he could ignore his need if he had to. Better to channel that energy into tomorrow's race. For now, he would sleep and rest, and then go fetch her at the appointed time. After that...well, he would just have to see.

Dammit, she needed to sleep. Bailey lay in her borrowed bed, eyes open and fixed on the ceiling, even though there wasn't much to see. Nasim might have provided power for the two lofts they occupied, and other locations as needed, but of course he hadn't done anything to light up the rest of downtown. The city was black as pitch under a moonless sky, desolate.

Haunted? Maybe, although she'd never believed in ghosts or anything that involved some kind of faith in the afterlife. Once you were done with your time on this planet, you were done forever. Even so, she'd had nights when she'd hidden in empty parking garages and could have sworn she heard whispers in the shadows, whispers that could have come from the souls who'd died of the Heat and then had the dust of their passing blown to who knows where on the wind.

This building wasn't haunted, though. No, the problem was that there seemed to be way too much life here, all concentrated in the lean, well-muscled form of the djinn next door.

The more she tried to forget that kiss, the exquisite warmth of Nasim's lips touching hers, it seemed the more it became indelibly burned into her mind. The way his hands had caressed her cheeks, his touch so tender, so gentle. She hadn't expected that from him. Although she'd done her best not to think of him in a sexual way at all, it had been impossible not to imagine what it might be like to be with him in bed. For some reason—possibly because of his supreme self-confidence—she'd thought sex with him would be hard and fast, without much time wasted on tenderness.

If that kiss was anything to judge by, she'd been dead wrong.

Stop thinking about it! she commanded herself, even though she knew that internal reprimand probably wasn't going to do much good. Even so, she had to try.

All right, she would think about the race tomorrow. Nasim's clothes had smelled of the wind and of pine needles and juniper and warm dry grass, so she was pretty sure they wouldn't be driving anywhere near downtown. Still, those plants grew wild all over Southern California. It wasn't as though she could use them to narrow down exactly where he'd set up his course. However, she could guess that the drive would probably be somewhere hilly, possibly a good ways outside L.A.'s downtown area. There were some pretty hairy roads that led up into the foothills in the San Gabriel Valley—Glendora Mountain Road, for one, and another up above La Cañada. It was hard to know for sure, since she didn't have any idea how careful he was going to be about staying close to home.

The GT-Rs would be good for that kind of racing; those cars had almost as much rear-end squat as the Porsche she'd been driving all these months. They were also great for straightaways, which was why she'd decided on them rather than a few other alternatives. Truth be told, the real reason she'd chosen that particular car was because she'd been itching to get her hands on one ever since she'd read about their latest redo in a copy of *Car and Driver*. That would have been a long shot at best; people like her generally didn't have the opportunity to drive a hundred-grand supercar whenever they felt like it.

But that had been in the old world. Now that Nasim could snap his fingers and conjure basically any car they wanted, she had the chance to drive vehicles that had only been wistful dreams in the past.

Maybe she should have made it best three out of five….

Is that because you would have gotten to drive more cars, or because you would get to spend more time with Nasim?

Bailey didn't want to consider that question, just as she didn't want to remember his kiss, those strong hands cupping her face. It was better to think about what she would do after she won. Nasim had said he would follow along as she drove to Los Alamos, just to make sure that none of the other djinn came after her, or he could take her there the way djinn traveled, with a simple snap of his fingers or blink of his eyes, or however that all worked. It would certainly be a lot faster than driving all those miles.

But then she wouldn't have a car. True, they'd probably have plenty of spare cars in Los Alamos, if the number of abandoned vehicles she'd seen in Los Angeles was any indication, but there were cars and there were *cars*. She'd hate to get stuck with someone's cast-off Prius, or whatever.

Well, she could figure that out when the time came. Right now, she had to focus on beating Nasim tomorrow. When she did....

"That's when you get to find out whether or not he's a man of his word," she said aloud as she continued to gaze up at the dim ceiling above her.

If it turned he wasn't...she really couldn't guess what she would do about that. But her wits hadn't failed her yet, and she knew she wouldn't allow them to betray her now, no matter what happened.

The next morning, Bailey was coolly businesslike when she appeared, black leather jacket back on despite the promised warmth of the day, her flaxen-pale hair once again gathered into a complicated braid. "You have them?" she asked.

"Down in the parking garage," Nasim replied. As much as he would have liked her to come to him and kiss him, reveal that she didn't want to race anymore, only wanted to stay here with him, he knew that wasn't likely to happen.

She nodded, then followed him as he led her down the stairwell into the building's tuck-under parking. The two GT-Rs were parked not too far from the entrance, one white, one a metallic charcoal gray.

"I'll take the white one," she said after giving them a brief glance.

"Of course," he replied, and reached in his pocket so she could take the key fob for the vehicle she'd requested. He was careful to leave it lying on his outstretched palm, because that way she couldn't accuse him of trying to get her to touch him in any way. After that kiss last night, she looked more guarded than ever, her gaze not quite meeting his. Right then, even though he'd enjoyed the embrace they'd shared, he wished he had held back, had shown more restraint. It was going to be difficult to get her to trust him again.

All those speculations would be rendered moot if she won, however, and so he knew he had to do whatever he could, short of cheating, to make sure he emerged the victor today. He needed her close in order to prove to her that he had no intention of getting her into bed and then abandoning her.

Actually, he wasn't quite sure what his intentions were yet, only that he wanted to make sure he didn't lose her.

"You can follow me," he said as she unlocked her vehicle. "It's some ways from here, so be prepared."

Her head cocked to one side. "How far?"

"Far enough."

Still giving him a dubious glance, she said, "You might as well go ahead and tell me. It's not like it's a state secret, right?"

Well, that was true. Nasim didn't quite know for sure why he was holding back, except that he had hoped he could make the location of their race a surprise. However, the last thing he wanted was for the two of them to get separated, because then Bailey would be in danger if any other djinn spotted her car, the only moving vehicle in an otherwise empty city.

"We're going to race along Mulholland Drive," he told her. "We'll start at Laurel Canyon and end at the merge with Coldwater Canyon. Do you know the route?"

She nodded. "Not well, but I know where it is. Do you want to get there by freeway, or surface streets?"

The freeway felt too exposed, so Nasim said, "We'll take surface streets. Beverly out of downtown, west to Crescent Heights. That will take us directly to Laurel Canyon."

"Okay. I'll follow you, but at least now I know where we're going."

Nasim supposed he should be relieved that Bailey didn't plan to pull out ahead of him so she could get to the starting point before he did. He wasn't sure what such a ploy would get her, but better to not have to worry about that scenario at all. "Let's go, then."

Without responding, she opened the door to her vehicle and got in, while he did the same. He'd already taken a little time to get used to the layout of the controls, which he supposed might be construed as cheating. However, even if Bailey hadn't driven one of these cars before, she obviously knew something about them, or she wouldn't have selected them as her vehicle of choice for their second race.

She was quick to follow him up the ramp that led out of the parking garage and onto the street, so it seemed he'd been correct about her familiarity with the GT-R. They went up to First Street and headed out of downtown, where the road became Beverly Boulevard after it stopped pointing north and jogged to the west. From there, it was an uneventful drive through mainly residential districts, with a brief distraction provided by a jaunt through what used to be a country club, the greens now nothing more than stretches of dry grass.

Although Nasim had studied maps of the area, he hadn't driven these streets himself. As they made their trek to Laurel Canyon, he marveled at the expanse of the city, at all the humanity that had once been packed into these few square miles. No one had been along to clear the streets in most of those neighborhoods, and so he and Bailey had to drive slowly, to thread their way through roads that were nearly blocked. Several times he had to wave a hand and move a wayward car or SUV up onto the sidewalk. He supposed he should have thought of this and come to clear the route he'd planned to take, but after all the effort he'd expended to make sure Mulholland Drive was open, he hadn't stopped to consider that his work had only been partly done.

Eventually, though, they were winding up through Laurel Canyon, leaving Hollywood and the central districts of Los Angeles behind. For whatever reason, this road appeared more open than the ones they'd just traversed, and only occasionally did they have to slow down to maneuver around a car or motorcycle or SUV. To either side were many grand houses, some of them hidden behind gates or hedges, some of them quite exposed to anyone traveling this route. This would have been a good place to settle as well, considering the views many of these houses must afford. However, if he had come here, he would not have found Bailey, which was his whole reason for taking a temporary residence in downtown Los Angeles.

Through it all, she was never more than twenty feet or so behind his rear bumper, slowing when he slowed, guiding the sleek white vehicle she drove around abandoned cars and trucks. He could just make out her face in his rearview mirror, her jaw set, her eyes shielded by a pair of dark sunglasses. Clearly, she was already focused on the competition yet to come.

At last they came to the intersection with Mulholland Drive, the left-hand side of which had been neatly designated with thick white bars painted on the asphalt, probably as a pedestrian crossing. The white lines also made for a handy starting point, though.

Nasim made the turn and then stopped with the nose of his car just barely over the white lines. Leaving the engine idling, he opened the door, got out, and walked over to Bailey's vehicle. She rolled down the window and peered out at him, gaze inquiring.

"It's a little less than two and a half miles to our destination," he said. "There's a thick white line painted on the road, then another, before the turn-off onto Coldwater Canyon. We'll use that as our finish line."

"All right," she replied. "Any other rules?"

"No," he said. "Fastest one there wins. However, if either of us tries to meddle directly with the other car, then the race is forfeit."

"No bumper cars. Got it—not that I would ever deliberately try to mess up one of these fine vehicles."

Nasim wondered whether he should be offended that she cared more about the welfare of the cars they were driving than about his own. Then again, Bailey probably assumed—and rightly so—that a djinn couldn't get hurt. She'd be putting herself far more at risk if she attempted that kind of maneuver.

"We're getting a late start," she went on. "Should we begin the race when our dash clocks get to twelve twenty-five?"

"That will be fine." He paused, then added, "Good luck."

A quick flash of a grin, one that made him wish he had the liberty to bend down and kiss her. "No, good luck to *you*. I think you're going to need it."

To that remark, he could only shake his head before he walked back over to his vehicle. He got in, fastened his safety harness, and looked at the digital clock on the dashboard.

Twelve twenty-three.

Full gas tank, engine idling but still giving him the same sensation of barely leashed power as the Ferrari. More so in a way, because the sound of this engine was bit gruffer, a bit lower pitched. It wanted to move, resented being made to wait like this.

Twelve twenty-four.

Nasim didn't dare allow himself to look over

at Bailey—not that he would have been able to see a great deal of detail through the tinted side windows of both vehicles. Instead, he kept his attention fixed on the dashboard, on the glowing numerals of the clock there.

Twelve twenty-five.

His head snapped back as he mashed his foot down on the accelerator. The engine roared, leaping forward with a speed that felt rather like he'd just been shot out of the world's largest cannon. Next to him, Bailey's car was a white blur, its nose nearly even with his. He was driving the wrong way, in the lane that should have been reserved for eastbound traffic, but it hardly mattered now, in a world as empty as this one was. The yellow line separating the lanes provided a guide of sorts, a clue as to how the road would twist and turn as it traveled along at nearly the summit of these hills.

Almost before he could blink, they'd arrived at the first curve in the road. Nasim let off the gas and allowed the car's transmission to automatically downshift, providing the torque to grind its way around the bend in their route, rear end sitting tightly with almost no oversteer. Good thing, because next to him Bailey was doing much the same thing, the white car slowing only enough to keep from slipping out of its lane.

The road straightened a little after that. Nasim

increased his speed, but just for a few seconds, because once again it curved, more shallowly this time, but in a series of three bends that didn't allow him any time to pump the gas, only to cling to the steering wheel as the GT-R hugged the road. Afterward, they came to another fairly straight stretch, Bailey beginning to pull ahead by a few inches.

Nasim gritted his teeth. Because he'd already been over this route, he knew they were coming up on yet another curve, one far sharper than the three they'd just traversed. He once again let off the gas and allowed the car to downshift, tires squealing in just the slightest bit of protest as he took the turn, the force of the de-acceleration pushing him back against the seat.

Next to him, Bailey wasn't quite as lucky. She obviously saw him begin to slow and did the same, but a fraction of a second too late. Tires screeched and smoke shot up from the asphalt as she corrected and pulled out of the turn—but now a good five or six feet behind him.

Excellent. Now all he had to do was maintain that lead.

The next couple of curves were shallower, so he took them at speed, pushing the car up to a hundred miles an hour and past it, the engine's growl now with a pleased note to it, as if it was glad to finally have a chance to show him what it could do.

In the rearview mirror, Bailey's white vehicle was beginning to inch forward, closing the gap between them by a foot or so. Although he didn't dare take his eyes off the road for more than a few seconds, Nasim could see the way her hands were clenched on the steering wheel, the determined set to her jaw. She didn't like being behind him, that was clear enough.

Well, she needed to get used to it, because he had no intention of allowing her to win a second time.

Shooting past the intersection with Skyline Drive now, and coming up on another sharp bend in the road. By now it felt like second nature to slow slightly, to let the engine downshift to keep its grip on the asphalt as it rocketed around the turn. It seemed that Bailey was picking up on the cues he offered, or maybe she was just getting used to the rhythm of Mulholland Drive, because she gained again on the curve, was now only a few feet behind him.

That wasn't good.

A few more turns, and then they came up to a fairly straight section, one where they both floored their accelerators. Bailey was now almost in his blind spot, which meant he was ahead by not much more than half a car length. Nasim found himself gritting his teeth, the leather-wrapped steering wheel damp under his palms. He couldn't let her win. If she did, he'd lose her forever.

Several more turns came next. Somehow Nasim managed to maintain his lead, but he didn't know how long that was going to last. The final straightaway was coming up, the one that would bring them to the intersection with Coldwater Canyon and the finish line. His only real chance was to mash the accelerator the second he came out of that last turn, and hope to hell that Bailey would be a little more conservative, since, unlike him, she had no idea that there were no more turns lurking ahead. The cars were both equipped with navigation systems, but because the satellites that once guided them were no longer transmitting, she wouldn't have been able to look up their route ahead of time.

Nasim had to hope it would be enough.

He rocketed past estates carefully hidden behind banks of trees and well-trimmed hedges, the speedometer now above 125 miles per hour and still climbing. Bailey dropped a little behind, but not by very much; if he'd had the energy to spare, he might have marveled at the way she was able to keep up despite being unfamiliar with the road.

The course was a little under two and a half miles long, but it felt as if they'd had been twisting and turning along Mulholland Drive for hours. Coming up was the final curve, the one that would bring them to the finish line. Nasim eased off the accelerator just enough to zip around the bend without leaving too much rubber on the road, while behind him, Bailey did the same.

It wasn't enough, though. Nasim's vehicle crossed over the thick white lines first, with the nose of Bailey's car even with his door handle. At once he hit the brakes, slowing to a stop before he ended up in the expansive yard of the house that faced the intersection.

Bailey did the same, and both cars came to rest in the middle of the road, smoke curling around them from their overtaxed tires. A pause, and then her car door opened and she climbed out. She was frowning, but in an abstracted sort of way, as if she was attempting to dissect her performance and figure out where things had gone wrong for her.

Nasim got out of his vehicle as well, doing his best to keep himself from smiling too much. Yes, this victory was a sweet one, but he saw no reason to rub it in.

"Nice cars," he said, hoping the comment was neutral enough that she wouldn't take offense.

"I'm glad you liked them," she replied. "Too bad mine wasn't fast enough."

"It was very fast. You were only behind me by less than a car length."

"Like I said, not fast enough."

She paused then, head tilted to one side as if attempting to catch a sound she could barely hear.

"What is it?" Nasim asked. Even as the question left his lips, however, he detected the same thing she had...a low growl.

Not from a wild animal, though. As they both stared southward along Coldwater Canyon, a bright green car with the Mercedes badge attached to its grille sped around the corner, then slammed on its brakes as soon as its driver seemed to catch sight of the two GT-Rs sitting in the middle of the intersection. The car came to a stop only a few feet from them. A few seconds later, the doors opened, and a man and a woman got out.

A human man and a djinn woman, Nasim corrected himself. He even thought he recognized her, although he didn't know her well. Fatima, the leader of the Bel-Air group of djinn and Chosen.

"Well, Nasim al-Jimir," she said. "What on earth are you doing here?"

TEN

Bailey didn't know who was more surprised to see the acid-green AMG Mercedes pull up and the man and woman climb out— Nasim, or herself. She had been certain that she and her djinn companion were the only two living beings in the Los Angeles area, but apparently not. Although nothing in Nasim's expression or posture indicated anything other than astonishment at being confronted by these newcomers, she couldn't quite hold back the shiver of disquiet that passed through her. While she had gotten somewhat used to Nasim, the prospect of facing any other djinn was worrying, to say the least.

One thing was for sure—she and Nasim weren't the only ones in L.A. with a sweet ride.

The woman was so strikingly beautiful that Bailey guessed she must be a djinn. For a moment, she thought the man with the djinn woman must also be an elemental, because he was amazingly good-looking, too. As she stared at him, though, Bailey realized he must be another mortal like herself, just model-pretty.

The question of what a djinn woman would be doing with a mortal man got shoved to the back of her mind, because the woman was addressing Nasim, addressing him by name, which meant they must know each other somehow.

"A friendly competition, Fatima," he said in response the woman's question as to what he was doing. "I thought we might as well put these empty roads to some use."

Fatima's kohl-circled dark gaze moved from Nasim to Bailey. "A competition with a human woman? But she is not your Chosen, is she?"

"No," he replied, posture somehow much more wary than it had been a few moments earlier. "Only someone to whom I've offered my protection."

The djinn woman frowned. "You know that is not allowed."

Allowed? Bailey could feel a frown of her own creasing her forehead. This Fatima was talking as though a certain set of rules existed for how humans and djinn should interact, and yet, as far as Bailey knew, the elementals' only interest in mortals seemed to be in how quickly they could kill them.

Well, true, Nasim wasn't like that. But there were undercurrents here she couldn't quite decipher. What was a Chosen, anyway, and why would Fatima use "your" to describe one, as though they somehow belonged to the djinn? Was that what this whole competition with Nasim was really about? If he won, would he own her in some strange sort of way?

Screw that, Bailey thought. *No one's going to own me.*

Apparently, Nasim wasn't too happy with Fatima's line of questioning, because when he replied, there was a distinct edge to his voice. "Are you my keeper, Fatima? What I do with my time is no concern of yours."

Rather than take offense, she only laughed a little, a sweet sound that had just a tinge of Glinda the Good Witch to it. "No, I am not your keeper. I only thought to give you a bit of friendly advice. You know the elders will not be happy when they find out what you are up to."

"Then that is between me and the elders," he said, his jaw tight. Obviously, he wasn't very happy at receiving this supposedly "friendly" advice. "So far, they have shown very little concern about what I have been doing. It seems that they are occupied elsewhere for the moment."

"I doubt their preoccupation will last forever," Fatima responded. "And at that time, you will need to explain yourself. But no matter. That is between you and the elders. If you do decide to make your companion your Chosen, then you are always welcome to join us in Bel-Air."

Nasim's blue eyes glinted. Bailey could tell he didn't think much of that suggestion. "Thank you for the invitation."

"You are most welcome. But I suppose that Adam—my Chosen—and I should go on with our drive. We do like to get out and about when we can."

"Mulholland is clear now," Bailey said, not sure precisely why she'd volunteered that information.

"Is it? Then I think we will go that way. The view is quite tremendous from up there."

She sent a bright smile at the two of them, then went back to her flashy green Mercedes and got in behind the wheel, her companion sending Nasim and Bailey an inquiring look before he climbed into the car as well. A million questions were bubbling in Bailey's mind, but she figured they needed to wait until she and Nasim were safely back at their lofts downtown.

"Well," she said, "what's the fastest way home?"

"'The fastest'?" he repeated. "This way, I suppose."

Before she could begin to react, he'd stepped close to her and put his arms around her waist. The world seemed to spin in all directions, and in the next second, they were standing in the living room of Nasim's loft.

"What the—?" Bailey shook her head, trying to clear it. The floor still didn't feel quite stable beneath her feet.

"That is how we travel," Nasim said, sounding far too calm, considering the whirlwind they'd apparently just ridden to get back to downtown.

The room had mostly stopped spinning. Bailey planted her hands on her hips and tilted her head at him. "What about the cars?"

"What about them?"

"You don't plan to just leave them there, do you?"

"Of course not. I've already sent them to the parking garage downstairs."

Of course he had. She hadn't even seen him snap his fingers, but apparently that wasn't a prerequisite for sending cars traveling halfway across L.A. in the blink of an eye. Every time she thought she'd come to terms with the enormity of his powers, he did something else to make her reevaluate exactly how immense they really were.

She said the first thing that came to her mind. "I need a drink."

At once, two glasses of red wine appeared in Nasim's hands. He came over to her and handed her one. "Here you are."

Actually, she'd been thinking of something a little stronger, like a good shot of whiskey, but she supposed this would do for now. Hand shaking a bit, she raised the glass to her lips and took a large swallow. That was better. Probably disrespectful of the wine, which as far as she could tell was more than decent, but right then she didn't care too much.

"Perhaps you should sit down."

A very good idea. Bailey went over to the couch, while Nasim took a seat on one of the low, gray-leather armchairs that faced it. With everything that had just happened, she'd almost forgotten the way he'd shellacked her in their race. All right, winning by a few feet probably didn't constitute a shellacking for most people, but it still annoyed the hell out of her. If she'd won today, then she wouldn't have to worry about elders, or Chosen—whatever they were—or much of anything else, because she'd be out of here.

As it was....

"Are you going to explain what all that was about?"

He didn't bother to ask what she meant by "all

that." A sip of wine, and then he said, "The elders aren't precisely our rulers, but they do make sure that we follow the rules, such as they are."

"What happens if you don't? You get put in djinn jail or something?"

Those questions elicited a thin smile without much humor in it. "Not exactly. For the worst crimes, there are what we call the outer circles, a region of the otherworld that makes your own Death Valley look like a tropical paradise. However, most of the time, it is only required that you correct whatever it is that you did wrong in the first place."

"And having me here like this is wrong somehow?"

"Yes."

"Why?"

"Because when it was decided that the djinn would reclaim this world, there were only two acceptable fates for humans. Death, or becoming Chosen."

That word again. "Which means what, exactly?"

"Those djinn who didn't agree with the fate humanity was about to suffer during the Heat were given the chance to save one human being, a human who would become that djinn's partner. Forever," Nasim added, in case the ramifications of that decision weren't entirely clear.

Bailey didn't speak for a moment, processing what Nasim had just told her. It was already pretty obvious that the djinn had caused the Heat somehow, so that part didn't surprise her very much. She was a little shocked that any djinn existed who were willing to saddle themselves with human partners for all eternity. Talk about your commitments.

That didn't seem to be what Nasim had in mind for her, though. As far as she could tell, he wanted the djinn equivalent of a fling, something they could both walk away from once they got tired of each other. Fine by her; she'd always known she wasn't the type to settle down. Sure, she'd cared for Diego, had been hurt and angry when Oscar interfered with that relationship, but even then she'd realized it wasn't something that was going to last for years. Really, it had been kind of stupid for Oscar to butt in, because if he'd just allowed matters to run their course, her relationship with his son probably would have been over in a few months—or at least no more than a year —anyway.

Of course, the only way Nasim would end up with her—even temporarily—was if he won their last race, and she wasn't about to let that happen.

"So Fatima was pissed off at you because you were hanging around with a human who wasn't your Chosen?"

"'Pissed off' might be a bit strong, but yes, she thought she needed to remind me of what all we djinn had agreed upon. I have no doubt she thought she was trying to be helpful."

More like a busybody. Bailey didn't see how it was Fatima's business what she and Nasim were up to. Maybe it was the elders' business—whoever they were—but since it sounded as though they were currently AWOL, they didn't seem to be too much of a threat, either.

"Well, I'm glad she didn't push it," Bailey said. "Our little agreement isn't any of her business."

"I agree." Nasim gazed at her for a moment, and she had to force herself to sit still, not to blink or do anything to reveal how uncomfortable she felt under that steady stare. There was something in his expression she couldn't quite read, something a bit too intense. "About that. Today's race was somewhat taxing. What if we take tomorrow off, and have our last competition the day after that?"

"I don't think it was taxing," she replied at once, although if forced to admit it to herself, she could tell this one had taken something out of her. The muscles in her shoulders ached from the way she'd hung onto the wheel and forced the car around all those dangerous curves and bends, reminding her that just because her collarbone was now healed, it didn't mean that the rest of her was entirely back to normal. Mulholland Drive had been a good choice of courses, but right then she found herself wishing Nasim had chosen something a bit less challenging. "I'm fine with racing tomorrow."

"And what if I'm not?" His tone was mild enough, and yet Bailey knew he was willing to dig his heels in on this particular point.

Fine. They'd take a day off, swim in the pool, lounge around. And she'd have to do whatever she could to avoid being in a position where he might try to kiss her again. Just the mere recollection was enough to send a little shiver through her body, but she knew she needed to be thinking with her brain and not her hormones. At least there wasn't any chance that Nasim would try to make her his Chosen and keep her around here forever. Even so, if he kissed her, tried something more than that, it could get into her headspace enough that she wouldn't be mentally prepared to defeat him in their final race. And she couldn't allow that to happen.

"You're a wimp?" she suggested before helping herself to another swallow of wine.

Luckily, he smiled at her remark, rather than taking offense at the epithet. "You can call me a wimp if you like. I still think it would be a good idea to give ourselves a bit of a rest."

"Okay, we'll have a rest." She drank more of

her wine, then set the glass down on the table. "What's your plan, then?"

Smile still in place, he replied, "I was thinking of a day at the beach."

———

Bailey had been reluctant at first, clearly surprised he would want to take her someplace so far out of their current orbit, but at length she had relented. "I could go for a little sand between my toes," she said.

An excursion to the beach was something of a calculated risk, but Nasim figured that, with so many miles of unoccupied coastline available right now, the odds of running into any other djinn were fairly low. He did not make the obvious choice and take them to Santa Monica, because it was possible that some of the Bel-Air djinn might have decided to take advantage of the fine weather and head down there themselves.

No, he brought Bailey to a hidden little cove near Corona del Mar, a place that was completely uninhabited now. Farther down the coast was the djinn and Chosen group in Laguna Beach, but since they had their own little piece of paradise right there, he doubted they would have any reason to come up here.

Pirate's Cove had only a few hundred feet of

actual beach, and was surrounded by rocky outcroppings that hid it from casual view. Getting here from the nearby beach at Corona del Mar itself was a bit of adventure, since the only way to reach the cove was to climb over those rocks.

Well, unless you happened to be a djinn.

They popped into existence in the middle of the white sand, Bailey still looking a little wild-eyed from the djinn mode of travel. However, she stepped away from Nasim as soon as their feet touched the sand and stood there, surveying their surroundings with her hands on her hips.

"Pretty," she said. "Where are we?"

"Pirate's Cove. Corona del Mar is just over those rocks." He pointed toward the large chunks of granite and sandstone that formed such an impressive barrier.

"Oh. I've never been here. Huntington, and Newport a few times, but I never came down to Corona."

"Well, you're here now."

She nodded, still gazing around at their surroundings, getting her bearings. Nasim had noticed how she always seemed to be on the alert, always made a note of where she was, what was happening around her. Probably a relic from so many months spent on the run, months where she could never allow herself to fully relax.

He hoped she could relax now.

For himself, he was doing his best not to stare at her. She'd traded her leather jacket, jeans, and plain dark T-shirt for the bikini he'd provided the day before, along with a spangled scarf wrapped around her waist. The little sequins flashed silver in the sun, but they weren't as bright as Bailey herself, her long blonde hair loose for once, full of little waves from the braid she usually wore.

He already considered her beautiful. Now, though, she was breathtaking.

"Some lunch?" he asked. As he spoke, a little cabana appeared on the sand behind him, with two chairs and a small table set between them, and a pitcher of sangria, a bowl of fresh fruit, and a plate of small sandwiches sitting on that table.

Bailey turned toward him and shook her head. "Everything is so easy for you djinn, isn't it?"

"I don't know about 'easy,'" Nasim replied, somewhat wounded by the insinuation that he'd never had to work hard at anything. "Our powers do allow us to perform tasks that would seem impossible to humans, but we still have our limitations."

"I haven't seen many yet," she remarked, then walked over to the cabana and sat down on one of the chairs inside.

"If I were all-powerful, I would have beaten you in both races." He came and sat down as well, then poured sangria into the glasses that waited for them.

"Maybe you threw the first race to make it seem as if I had a chance." She picked up a glass and took a sip, but her gaze remained on his face, speculative.

Nasim didn't know whether he should be offended at her suggestion that he would cheat, or flattered that she considered him such a good driver that he could have beaten her twice in a row. "I assure you, I did no such thing. Those were both true tests of our driving skill."

"If you say so." With her free hand, she reached for one of the little sandwiches, this one of chicken salad with sliced grapes and nuts, and took a bite. After washing it down with some sangria, she went on, "If you put that little defeat aside, it seems as if you can do pretty much anything you want to."

"Mostly," he admitted. "Except when it comes to those things controlled by the elements. Mine is air, and so I can call the winds to me, or fly, but I cannot cause an earthquake, or make the tide come in any more quickly. All of this"—he gestured toward the cabana where they sat, and the food on the table between them—"is just a matter of imagining those things I need, and having them come to me. It's not exactly like making them appear out of thin air."

"I think you're splitting hairs on that one, Nasim."

He smiled at her. "It might sound like that to you, but there is a subtle difference. These things already exist somewhere in the world—the grains for the bread, the wine, the fruit. I just have to bring them here and combine them in the way I want."

For a moment, Bailey didn't reply, only seemed to consider his words as she chewed thoughtfully. "I guess I can see how that would work. It does seem mostly like magic, though."

"I suppose that's as good a word for it as any." Nasim reached for his glass of sangria and drank, glad of the cool, fruity taste. They were sheltered from the sun here inside the cabana, but the day itself was still warm and bright, promising to be actually hot. The fog of a few days ago seemed like a distant dream.

As did his days before he met Bailey. They had been in each other's lives for a very short time, and yet he felt more comfortable with her than he had with many women of his own kind. She had a toughness he admired, an unwillingness to give up no matter how much the odds might be stacked against her. He admired that just as much as he admired her bright beauty, the lushness of her body.

Although right now he had to admit that the

curve of her breasts in that meager bikini top was more than a little distracting.

"It does feel good to get out, though," she said, watching the sunlight dance on the waves as they crested and broke against the shore. These were not the large breakers of the main beach, but delicate miniatures of their bigger cousins, topped with lacy foam. "I mean, I know we were out earlier, but this feels different."

"We were still in Los Angeles." Nasim picked up a slice of apple and took a bite. "Now we've left it behind."

She was silent for a moment, gaze still fixed on the water. Without looking at him, she said, "The other day, you said you'd come to L.A. to hunt me."

"I'm not sure I would put it so baldly, but yes."

"If you came to Los Angeles for that reason, then you must have started out someplace else. Where do you live? I mean, *really* live?"

A good question. Before the Heat, he had dwelled in a palace in the otherworld, just as all his kind did. But then the Earth became their home, with each of them given a certain plot of land to make their own. Despite being granted a particularly lush piece of property in Napa, it still did not feel particularly his. However, he supposed that it was, in Bailey's phrasing, the place where he "really lived."

"My lands are to the north of here, in a place called Napa. To be specific, at what used to be the Chateau Montelena winery."

Now she turned away from her inspection of the waterline, eyebrows raised slightly. "You live in a chateau?"

"They called it a chateau. I suppose it looks rather like one, from the outside at least. But it was a true functioning winery."

"If it's really a winery, shouldn't you be looking after your grapes instead of lounging on the beach?"

The question had a teasing note to it, so Nasim didn't take any great offense. "The leaves have finished sprouting, and the fruit won't be coming for a few more weeks yet. This was a good time to let them be. Later in the season, yes, they will need some looking-after."

"A winery." She shook her head. "That's a new one."

"Not really. We djinn do love our wine, and once the current stores have been used up, then we will need to make more." True enough, and yet Nasim still had to wonder why the elders had given him the former winery as his home. It was not as if he had ever evinced any great interest in horticulture in general or viticulture in particular.

Yes, he had possessed carefully tended container gardens of earthly plants and flowers in the courtyards of his palace in the otherworld, but the same could be said for many other djinn. He was certainly not so very unusual in that regard.

"I guess you're right." That teasing glint was back in Bailey's blue eyes. "Do you know anything about winemaking?"

"No. I suppose I shall have to learn by trial and error." He paused, taking note of the amused quirk to her lips. "It will be something to do with my time. And, as I said before, it is a very beautiful place."

Her gaze returned to the water. "So is this."

Nasim couldn't argue with her on that point. The sky overhead was the same brilliant blue as her eyes, the water below nearly as clear and sparkling. The wind was fresh and clean, overlaid with the sharp tang of salt. Seagulls wheeled and cried above them, a counterpoint to the ever-present murmur of the sea.

"That is why I wished to bring you here," he said. "It is always good to have a change of scenery every once in a while."

"Like what Fatima and her boy-toy were doing."

"Her Chosen," Nasim said, taking care to keep his tone mild. Actually, Bailey's epithet for the young man was accurate enough. He certainly had been very pretty, perhaps one of the main reasons why Fatima had selected him in the first place. However, Nasim had to hope the mortal possessed brains that were at least something of a match for his looks, or he feared Fatima might find herself bored with her companion sooner rather than later.

But that really was not his problem. Even so, he found himself thinking that he would probably never get bored with Bailey.

You will have no need to get weary of her, he told himself. *For if you win your next race and take her back with you to Napa, you will only spend as much time with her as you both agree upon.* And afterward? Well, he would still owe her respect and admiration, even if he could not give her his love, and so of course he would make sure she had a safe journey to New Mexico. It would be the least that he could do for her.

"He can be a boy-toy and her Chosen at the same time," Bailey pointed out, which seemed sensible enough that Nasim did not bother to contradict her. "Anyway, it sounded as if they went out driving a lot. Do you think others in their community go to the beach very much?"

"Probably. Although Bel-Air is where they are required to live, I believe they can venture out and about as long as they don't attempt to settle anywhere else."

"Rough life," Bailey remarked after taking a sip of her sangria. "Confined to Bel-Air for all eternity."

Nasim chuckled. "I suppose there are worse fates."

Almost at once Bailey's expression darkened, although she didn't reply immediately, only sipped again from her glass of sangria. He thought he could guess at the reason for her change in demeanor—no doubt she was thinking of all those who had died from the Heat, or suffered far more painful deaths at the hands of the djinn reavers. Those were all much worse fates than being confined to Bel-Air forever. Unfortunately, he couldn't think of anything to say that would make her feel better. He couldn't change what had happened. All he could do was attempt to keep her safe.

He set down his own glass. "I think I shall go in the water now."

Bailey tilted an eyebrow at him. "Aren't you supposed to wait half an hour after eating before you go swimming? Or do djinn not have to worry about that sort of thing?"

"I don't think either of us have eaten enough for it to be a problem one way or another." Nasim got up from his chair and walked down to the waterline. A little wave passed over his foot. The water was colder than he had expected, much colder than the water in his rooftop swimming pool. Still, he thought he should get used to it soon enough.

He waded out into the clear water of the cove, moving past the spot where the waves broke so he could float on his back in a spot where the movement of the water was a bit more serene. This was better; the sun beat down on him, and danced in little glittering sparks all around.

A moment later he heard the sound of splashing, and realized Bailey had left her seat in the cabana to join him out here in the water. Little waves rippled around him, and then there she was, fair hair floating on the current like some kind of fairy-tale seagrass.

"Damn, it's cold," she said, treading water a few feet away. "I always forget that about the beach. It looks like it should be so much warmer, but it's not."

"I will admit that it's far from tropical."

"Maybe we should've stayed in L.A. and gone swimming in the pool."

Nasim shifted, feet sinking down so he no longer floated on his back. Bailey hadn't moved, was still almost but not quite within arm's reach. Had she done that so he wouldn't feel tempted to take her by the hand and pull her toward him? If so, she had miscalculated, because he could be next to her quickly enough if he so desired.

"You really think so?" he asked, glancing around at the white sand of the beach a few yards away, the sheltering rocks, that particular quality of light one only seemed to find at the ocean, shimmering and lustrous and bright.

A pause, and then she sent him a rueful smile. "I guess not. This is good. It almost feels like…." And her words trailed off as though she realized she shouldn't complete the thought.

"Almost feels like what?" he probed.

"Like it never happened. Like if we left this cove, the world would be back the way it was." Her gaze shifted away from him, toward the small private beach. "Although deep down I know that if things were really back the way they had been, then that beach would be packed full of people."

Before he realized what he was doing, he had paddled with his feet, pushing him closer to her. To his relief, she didn't move away, only looked at him with a curious mixture of sorrow and confusion in her big blue eyes. He said, "I wish I could make things the way they were."

"Do you?"

"Mostly." Nasim paused, searching for the right words, not sure if they even existed. "As long as you and I could also be together in that world."

He reached for her hand, pulled her close. She didn't try to get away, came to him willingly enough. In the next moment, their lips were touching, their bodies pressed together. Despite the cold water, he knew he was beginning to harden, wondered if she could feel it.

If she did, she didn't seem to mind, for she made no move to pull away. She tasted of salt-water and sweet sangria, and Nasim thought he had never experienced anything so delicious in his life.

The kiss lasted a long time. At last, though, she seemed to shake her head, to make a sound low in her throat that wasn't quite a "no" but was close enough. Her hands, which had been clutching his shoulders, now instead pushed against his chest, creating enough distance between them that she was able to keep swimming, now headed for the shore.

He let her go. What other choice did he have? Never in his life had he forced a woman, and he certainly was not about to start now. Clearly, Bailey wanted him but couldn't quite come to terms with her desire. That was probably why she had agreed to their wager in the first place—she wouldn't allow herself to be with him willingly, but if she lost, she could still indulge her need without admitting it was something she had wanted for herself.

Very well. When they met for their last race, he would just have to make sure there was no chance of her winning.

ELEVEN

Damn it. She had sworn she wouldn't let Nasim kiss her again, and yet there she was, lip-locking with him in the middle of Pirate's Cove, of all places. His mouth had been as warm as the water was cold, and she'd felt that same thrill of heat within her, the one which told her all too clearly that she wanted a lot more than just a kiss.

There was a small table with a stack of towels off to one side of the cabana. Bailey hadn't noticed it before, but she guessed that Nasim had conjured it as she was grimly wading to shore. It was a small, considerate note...or was it? Maybe all he really wanted to do was impress her with his thoughtfulness.

Right then, she didn't know what to think.

Mouth compressed, she began toweling herself off, then reached over for the sequined scarf she'd been using as a sarong and wrapped it around her waist once she was sure she was sufficiently dry to keep her damp bikini bottoms from damaging the pretty fabric. As she worked, Nasim came ashore and stood a few paces off, water trickling down his muscled chest and stomach, his strong legs.

Don't look, she told herself. *Because him standing there and looking like a Greek god isn't going to do anything for your head.*

"I think we should discuss this," he said.

"What's to discuss?" she asked. "We both lost control. Again."

Without speaking, he went past her into the cabana and got a towel for himself. Silently, he dried himself off, then folded the towel and set it down on the edge of the table. "Is it losing control when it's something we clearly both want?"

"It may be clear to you. It's not to me."

To her surprise, he chuckled. "How much clearer does it need to be? I barely have to reach out a hand to you, and you're in my arms."

Oh, for fuck's sake. "Screw you, Nasim," she said distinctly, then marched out of the cabana and headed toward the rocks that sheltered the cove from the rest of the beach. The way up and out was clear enough, and she figured she should be able to manage it, even barefoot as she was.

As quickly as she walked, however, he was

right there beside her. "Where do you think you're going?"

"Away from you."

His fingers closed on her wrist. Not roughly, but with a firm enough grip that she knew she'd have difficulty getting away. "You know that's not safe," he said. There was no anger in his tone or his expression; disappointment, yes, but nothing else except possibly fear for her well-being. "You are barefoot. You don't have a vehicle. And I cannot guarantee that there aren't other djinn in the area, others who will not care as much about your safety as I do."

"If you cared so much, would you be challenging me to races like the one we just ran earlier today?"

"Is that it?" He stepped closer, so close Bailey could smell the scent of saltwater rising from his smoothly tanned skin. A little shiver passed over her, and she swallowed. It really wasn't fair that he should be so completely overwhelming. "We both agreed to the terms of our bargain. I thought you enjoyed racing."

"I do. I just—"

"Just what?"

She wasn't about to tell him that she only enjoyed it when she won, because that wasn't the whole truth. The experience of pushing a fast car to its limits always excited her, whether or not she emerged the victor. No, what she'd hated about the race today was realizing that there was a real possibility she might lose, might have to stay here with Nasim. She didn't want to belong to him, even temporarily. That thought frightened her more than anything else.

Well, almost anything else. Her deepest fear, the one she didn't want to drag kicking and screaming into the light, was that she would enjoy being with him too much, would realize that a solitary existence—despite the freedoms it offered —wasn't quite as satisfying as she wanted it to be. Her fierce attraction to Nasim was unlike anything she'd ever experienced before, and she didn't know what to do about it.

Better to walk away before she really got in over her head.

"I want to race tomorrow," she said. "I don't want to wait. I want this over with."

Almost at once his eyes went shuttered, heavy dark brown lashes hiding the cloudy blue. He hadn't wanted to hear her say that, she could tell. He wanted her to say it was all right for them to take another day off, so he could wine her and dine her and maybe do his best to get her into bed. If that happened, then she would be conflicted, wouldn't be focused on winning…or at least, she guessed that was probably his line of reasoning.

Well, that wasn't going to happen.

He drew in a breath. "If that is what you wish."

"It is."

"Then we will go back so you can prepare."

Before she could even blink, his arms had gone around her waist again. Not to embrace her, or to try to kiss her, but so he could take her away from the beach and back to her loft in downtown Los Angeles. It was there that they rematerialized, and not in Nasim's condo.

The significance of that choice wasn't lost on her.

"Thanks," she said, and he only lifted his shoulders.

"It's what you asked for. You choose the venue, I choose the cars. I will meet you in the lobby at ten minutes until noon tomorrow."

He whisked himself away, disappearing with that disconcerting little *pop* of air that seemed to accompany all the djinns' magical comings and goings. Almost at once, Bailey wished she could have said something to soften her rejection just a little, because she could tell he was angry with her, but the moment had come and gone.

Besides, why should *she* be apologizing? He was the one who'd forced himself on her.

No, that was being unfair. She'd *wanted* the kiss. That was the whole problem. If she'd been reluctant, then she could have just called him out for being an asshole djinn he-man and felt absolutely guilt-free about pushing him away.

But she'd wanted him to kiss her, and now she was feeling like a total bitch for giving him the shove-off, and all in all, this was just a delightful end to the day, even though it was still just mid-afternoon.

Bailey wandered into the kitchen and poured herself a glass of water. Probably the best thing to do was take a shower, get all that ocean salt off her. Maybe then she'd feel a little better about the whole situation.

Thus resolved, she headed into the bathroom, peeled off her damp bikini, and climbed into the shower, turning up the water as hot as she dared. And no, she wasn't going to think about having Nasim in there with her, because that kind of defeated the whole purpose of doing her best not to think about him, but rather to start working on ideas for their race the next day.

Unfortunately, the more she tried not to think about him, the more he invaded her thoughts. This would all have been a lot easier if she didn't like him so much.

And that realization made Bailey want to shake her head at herself. She never thought she'd see the day when she could say she actually liked a djinn. The entire notion should have been utterly abhorrent. After all, the djinn had destroyed the world, slaughtered almost every man, woman, and child. She would have been the first to admit back in the day that there were some choice specimens of humanity who deserved to be killed off without mercy, but even in her blackest moods, she would never have said that *all* of humanity deserved to die.

But now here she was, playing kissy-face with one of the immortals who'd been behind that annihilation, or at least had gone along with it, and she really must be losing her damn mind.

Teeth gritted, she rinsed the conditioner out of her hair, washed the rest of herself off, and got out of the shower stall. Once she was dressed again in some jeans and a T-shirt, her hair blotted to near-dryness, she felt a little more like herself. Time to get thinking.

She poured herself another glass of water and went to stand by the window, not because she was looking for anything in particular, but because she hoped staring at downtown L.A.'s outlines might help her to figure out the scope of the all-important third and final race. They'd drag-raced and street-raced, and so she didn't much see the point in revisiting either of those kinds of contests. Yes, of course a new race would be subtly different even if it was the same general type, simply because they'd be in a new venue and driving different cars. Still, that didn't seem to be enough.

Her gaze shifted toward the mountains east of downtown. Not that she was considering driving there—it would only be a revisit of their race this morning on Mulholland—but because an idea flashed into her mind, one that probably should have gotten there sooner, considering the place she had in mind was where she'd been working when she first met Oscar.

Auto Club International Speedway.

They could have a circle-track match-up, a set number of laps. Whoever got to the finish line on the final lap would win. It was simple, and perfect. The only problem might be whether there were any of the evil, reaver djinn in the area, but Bailey supposed that Nasim would check it out first to make sure the coast was clear. Fontana didn't seem like the kind of place where any of the elementals would have settled, considering they seemed to end up at wineries or in ritzy suburbs, but again, that was something Nasim could check. That meant she'd have to tell him about her choice before their designated meeting time the next morning. Well, she could always fall back on the old note under the door trick. She'd wait until around 10 a.m. and let him know then. That would give him enough time to scope out Fontana and its environs, and it would probably be after he'd chosen their cars. It was possible that he'd change his mind and get them something else to drive once he realized what she had in mind, but she'd just have to take that risk.

The matter settled, Bailey felt a bit better. Not all the way better, because she couldn't help thinking about Nasim and what he might be doing in that suspiciously quiet loft next door, but enough that she could heat up a slice of pizza and eat it without feeling as though she was going to puke from anxiety.

One step at a time.

Alone in his loft, Nasim had to repress the urge to punch his fist through the wall, partly because such a display wouldn't gain him anything in the end, and partly because the walls of this building were made of solid brick and that kind of gesture would have hurt like a bastard, even with all his djinn powers of regeneration.

Instead, he summoned the pitcher of sangria and the plates of sandwiches and fruit they'd left behind at the cabana, and poured himself another drink and helped himself to a chicken salad sandwich. Every ounce of his being wanted to go next door and have this out with Bailey, but his instincts told him that would be a spectacularly bad idea. If she wanted to push him away, so be it. He would concentrate on making sure he won their race tomorrow. She might be prickly and closed off and difficult, but she would never go back on a bet. If she lost, she wouldn't try to wriggle out of their deal.

Very well, then. He tried to imagine what kind of race she would dream up for their final confrontation. Something he wasn't expecting, probably. Once again, images of dune buggies racing across the Mojave Desert danced his head, but he pushed them away. That sort of race required too specialized a vehicle. He supposed they could race dune buggies on the street, but the reverse wasn't true; he couldn't see a couple of Lamborghinis trying to struggle their way across Death Valley.

No, he was fairly certain that whatever she was dreaming up, it would take place on pavement. Between the Porsches and the Ferraris and the high-end Nissans, they'd already covered a fairly respectable range of powerful vehicles, but he guessed there were plenty more where those had come from. The trick was to figure out which type of race Bailey would decide on.

For research, he conjured some back issues of various car magazines, and beamed a few episodes of *Top Gear* and *Grand Tour* into the loft's television set. That helped to kill a few hours, but, more importantly, the magazine articles and the TV shows helped him determine that there was one vehicle they definitely needed to drive for their final showdown.

The McLaren P1.

Fewer than four hundred of the last model year had been built before the Heat wiped out anyone who could create another one. That meant the cars were far less thick on the ground than even the Ferraris he and Bailey had driven in their first race. In all of California, he could locate only one of the vehicles he sought; he had to reach out all the way to Scottsdale in Arizona to find another, and bringing it here required an expenditure of energy he hadn't really planned on. Once it was tucked safely away in the underground parking garage, Nasim ate the rest of the sandwiches on the plate, then downed another glass of wine.

After he'd replenished his stores of energy somewhat, he felt a bit better. Good thing that he would be completely recovered by the time their final race occurred, because he could tell he would need every ounce of his concentration to wrestle with the beast of a car he'd summoned. Deep down, he wondered if he might have gone too far, might have decided on a vehicle he had no hope of mastering, but Nasim told himself that Bailey would probably face much the same set of problems when she found herself behind the wheel of the P1. She had a great deal of driving experience, true, but he very much doubted she had ever driven a car like this. They should be equally matched.

The thought crossed his mind that perhaps he should take the McLaren out for a test drive, and almost as quickly he rejected the notion. It seemed a bit too much like cheating to him, giving himself an advantage when Bailey would not have the same opportunity. Also, he couldn't know for sure how watchful she was being, and he didn't want to risk her catching a glimpse of him exiting the parking garage in the P1. He didn't want to spoil the surprise. True, she might attempt to sneak into the garage to see what sort of cars he'd summoned, but he'd made sure the entry from the stairwell was locked tight with his djinn magic, as was the gate that guarded the ramp which led to street level. It wasn't that he didn't trust her, exactly, just that he thought it was better to be safe.

Anyway, dusk had fallen on the city by now, and as conspicuous as the McLaren might be during the daylight hours, it would be doubly so once it was truly dark and he had to switch on the headlights. At least he had read accounts written by people who had driven the car, and he had watched the episode where the big, burly man who seemed in charge of the *Grand Tour* show had taken it for a few laps around the track. His reactions had already given Nasim some of the information he needed—that the P1 was monstrously powerful and awesomely quick, and that he needed to treat it with the respect it deserved and never let his guard down for a moment.

Nasim went over to the wall that separated his loft from Bailey's and stood there quietly, listening, but he couldn't hear anything. It was far too early for her to have gone to sleep, and she didn't have the ability to make any television show she wanted appear for her watching pleasure. He supposed she might be reading—he had seen books and magazines in the loft she was using—although he had to admit to himself that she didn't seem like the reading type. Perhaps she was eating, sitting alone at the stark white table in the loft's dining area.

That image saddened him. He wished he could go over and sit down at the table with her, reach over and take her hand. Unfortunately, her rejection from earlier that day had been all too clear. No matter how much she might react to him—and he could tell she did, knew that her desire was almost as strong as his, even if she did her best to ignore it—he also knew she was determined to get away from him. Her stubbornness and need for independence refused to allow her to understand that in this case, being alone was not her best course of action.

Very well. He would just have to prove to her that she did belong with him, if only so they both might amuse themselves for a season or two.

First, though, he had a race to be won.

TWELVE

Somehow, she'd managed to sleep, probably because she knew that tossing and turning and replaying that scene in Pirate's Cove wouldn't do her any damn good, would only make her less ready for her race with Nasim. And that morning she'd gotten up and calmly showered and gotten dressed, had eaten her breakfast and drunk her coffee and brushed her teeth, had done all the things a person should do while getting ready for their day. Inside, though, she felt as tightly drawn as a bowstring, ready to snap at a moment's notice. So much was riding on this.

It didn't help that there was nothing much in the loft to keep her occupied, except those useless old copies of *Forbes* and *Architectural Digest* she'd noticed earlier. More than once, she went to the window to check the skies outside; rain in May in

Southern California was very rare, but a heavy fog could make the asphalt damp and slick.

However, the day looked as cheerfully sunny as the one before had, without a single cloud to break the expanse of bright blue overhead. Bailey supposed that was a good sign, but even so, she couldn't prevent her anxiety from ratcheting up higher and higher. However this turned out, she wanted it over with. She hated feeling unsettled, not sure of what was coming next. Probably a shrink would have told her that was just a relic of her childhood, when she could never be certain of where she was going to call home, who she was going to end up with next. That might even be true, but knowing it was the truth didn't help her much in the here and now.

At ten o'clock, she exited her loft, checked the hallway to make sure it was empty—although why Nasim would be loitering there, she had no idea—and slipped the piece of paper with the location of their next race written on it under the door. Her heart pounded, and she worried he was going to open that door and ask her what the hell she was doing, but she managed to get back inside her own place without being accosted. Maybe he was in the shower.

At any rate, he didn't come over to ask any questions, and at last it was a quarter to noon. Bailey headed out of her loft and went downstairs to the lobby, where Nasim was already waiting for her. He wore his usual uniform of a dark T-shirt and jeans; she wondered if he'd adopted that outfit because it was comfortable, or because he was trying to put her at ease, make her think he really wasn't all that different from her.

A little late for that, she thought. *I know what you are.*

But even as the thought crossed her mind, she recalled the sensation of his lips touching hers, those strong arms holding her close. He hadn't felt like some otherworldly creature. He'd felt like a man.

He wasn't, though, and she knew she'd just have to keep reminding herself of that fact until it finally got drilled into her thick brain.

"Good morning," he said, his tone stiff, formal, at odds with his casual attire. It seemed pretty obvious that he hadn't forgiven her for bailing on him yesterday.

Well, that was fine by her. She didn't need his forgiveness.

"Morning," she echoed.

Still wearing that unsmiling expression, he said, "I went to look at this Auto Club Speedway of yours. The area around it is empty. No one should interfere with what we plan to do."

For some reason, Bailey didn't feel quite as relieved by his words as she'd thought she would be. Maybe it was simply that she had to take his word for it that the area was safe, although she had to admit to herself that he hadn't lied to her so far. "So, you saw that it was an oval track, right?"

He nodded.

"We'll race a certain number of laps, and whoever crosses the finish line first, wins. We won't have a checkered flag or anything, but we've done okay without one so far."

"True," he said. "No need to be formal. Well, then, let's go down to the garage so you can see what you'll be driving today."

Without waiting for her to respond, he turned and headed down the stairwell. Bailey refused to be offended, mostly because she was doing her best to tell herself that she couldn't help it if she'd hurt his feelings. Maybe he'd think twice before he went and pawed the next unsuspecting woman.

All right, he hadn't exactly pawed her. She'd been a willing participant. But he really needed to get his head out of his ass and realize she wasn't going to go any farther than the two kisses they'd shared.

All thoughts of Nasim's wounded ego went flying out the window as soon as Bailey exited the stairwell and saw the two gleaming, low-slung vehicles waiting for them there. One was pure black, dark as night, and the other was chrome yellow with black accents. They both looked deadly as hell, and that wasn't any mere façade—handled improperly, those cars could send you into the next life while you were still blinking and trying to figure out what had gone wrong.

"McLaren P1s," she breathed.

"You like them?"

"They're—" She broke off there, fairly certain that her vocabulary didn't possess the words needed to express how she felt about the supercars parked only a few feet away from where she stood. "Where the hell did you get them?"

"A dealership in Newport Beach, another in Scottsdale."

"Do you have any idea how much these cars are worth?"

Nasim shrugged. "Yes. One point two-five million dollars each. Not that it really matters now, does it?"

No, it probably didn't. Money wasn't worth anything anymore, not when you could walk onto a lot and drive off with whatever car you wanted, or hole up in a ten-million-dollar compound in Malibu. Of course, that shelter probably wouldn't last for very long once the djinn got wind of you, but still. Bailey had never cared much about the trappings of wealth—probably because she'd never had any—but she knew there had been ample opportunity for her to loot the jewelry stores in

L.A.'s Diamond District, if that had been her thing. She could have raced around downtown in her sports car while wearing a million dollars' worth of ice, had she cared to.

Because she hadn't cared, all that fancy jewelry remained where it was. The only thing she'd cared about was having a fast car that would keep her safely ahead of any pursuing djinn.

Well, she was looking at an extremely fast car right now. Whether it would keep her away from Nasim remained to be seen.

"You're right—it doesn't matter," she said. "Still, these are cars you need to treat with respect. Nine hundred horsepower…660 lb-ft of torque… it's not exactly like driving your mother's minivan."

One of Nasim's eyebrows assumed an ironic tilt. "I am fairly certain my mother never drove a minivan."

"You know what I mean."

He flashed her a smile, the kind that made her knees feel the tiniest bit wobbly. Somehow, Bailey knew he'd deployed that smile like a weapon, not because he was genuinely amused. He wanted her to feel off-balance as they started their race.

Nice try, she thought. *I've had people playing head games with me since before I could walk. But better luck next time.*

"I used some maps to guide me to the racetrack," he said. "I already know where we're going."

"But you don't know how to drive there," Bailey objected. She paused, remembering how they'd snaked their way across L.A.'s empty streets to get to Mulholland Drive. "Those cars are going to be pretty conspicuous, driving all that way on a freeway with no one else on it. If it turns out there are any djinn in the area, aren't we going to attract their attention?"

"Oh, we won't be driving there," he said calmly. "I'll send the cars over, and then I will take you with me in the normal djinn way."

That made some sense, although the last thing Bailey wanted was to give Nasim the opportunity to hold her as closely as he needed to while traveling djinn-style. Still, it would be much safer than driving the whole way.

She really didn't want to think about the enormous amount of power required to send two cars from downtown Los Angeles to Fontana in the blink of an eye. Yes, he'd done the same thing over greater distances just to get the cars here in the first place, but she figured he must have transported each one separately, rather than summoning them here in tandem. And that didn't even count the energy he'd have to expend to get himself and Bailey to the racetrack.

"Okay," she said, hoping she sounded firm

and not worried at all. "That does sound like it would be safer."

He nodded, staring down at the cars for a moment. His eyes shut for a moment, and first the all-black McLaren, and then the chrome-yellow one, blinked out of existence. They made the same popping noise that Nasim himself made when he disappeared, only much louder, probably because more air was being displaced.

When he reopened his eyes, he said, "It's done."

"Just like that?" Bailey asked, even though she'd seen for herself the way the cars had vanished into nothingness. Then again, it wasn't as though she'd seen where they *went*.

"Just like that. Now it's our turn."

Trying not to seem too reluctant, Bailey stepped toward him, held herself still as he put his arms around her waist. He smelled fresh and clean from the shower he must have taken earlier that morning, and she had to force herself to focus on something other than his nearness, anything but the sensation of those strong arms holding her, the warmth of his flesh.

She couldn't be distracted now.

One of those eye-blinks, and the underground parking garage was gone, replaced by the infield of the speedway. It was partially filled with aban-doned vehicles, and she had to remind herself that parking had been permitted there during certain events. But the mountains in the background were still the same, as was the line of palm trees that still grew off to one side. They had survived humanity's demise, probably because they didn't need regular care.

However, worries about the palm trees evaporated as soon as she saw the two P1s parked on the track, not too far from the starting line. Nasim let go of her. "Shall we?"

She nodded, not sure she trusted herself to speak. Between trying to banish the sensation of his arms around her and her worry about the upcoming race, her throat felt tight, her stomach twisted into knots.

Shake it off, she told herself. *You can do this.*

When they stopped next to the cars, Nasim asked, "Which one would you like?"

"The black one," she replied immediately. She'd never been a fan of yellow.

"Very well." He extended an outstretched hand to her. On his palm rested an electronic key fob. "Here you are. We'll have to drive to the starting line, since I didn't get the vehicles oriented exactly."

"That's fine," Bailey said. "That'll give us both a little time to get used to the cars."

"True enough. Shall we?"

"Sure."

They walked side by side until they reached the cars, and then Nasim went ahead and climbed into the black and yellow vehicle. Bailey went to her own car and got in, trying to reassure herself that this was just another sports car, and there wasn't anything she needed to worry about, even though every muscle in her body was taut as a harp string and nervous sweat trickled down her back.

Nothing to worry about. Right.

A moment to get her harness and mirrors adjusted, another to let her eyes skim the controls, doing her best to take a crash course on the McLaren's interior. Exposed carbon fiber on the dash and door trim, an all-electronic display that showed an outline of the vehicle, calling out tire pressure and fuel levels and a whole host of things she probably wouldn't have time to read once the race got under way. The steering wheel felt thick under her fingers, although she hoped she would get used to it quickly enough. And there was the switch that enabled "race mode," allowing her to lower the car's body and increase the spring stiffness, something designed for exactly the kind of driving she'd be doing in the next few minutes.

She started the engine and sucked in a breath at the deep growl of the motor, the feeling that this thing could hurl her right into orbit if she wasn't careful. It was strange, because both the

Ferrari and the Porsche she'd driven recently had enormous amounts of torque as well, and yet she hadn't gotten the same impression of utter raw power that she did from the P1.

It's okay, baby, she thought at the car. *You take care of me, and I'll take care of you.*

Nasim had already begun to guide his vehicle to the starting line. Holding her breath, Bailey put her foot on the accelerator. To her surprise, the McLaren moved sedately enough from the spot where it had been parked, but that was probably because she had applied very little pressure to the gas pedal. The power was still there, just coiled, waiting.

Soon.

The starting line was only about fifty yards or so away. It didn't take very long to get there. Once she put the P1 in park, Nasim got out of his car and came over to her. "Would you like to start at 12:15?"

"That's fine." *Just four minutes from now....*

"How many laps?"

Bailey glanced away from him and scanned the track as it stretched before her. NASCAR races run here at the Auto Club Speedway had taken two hundred laps, but there was no way she would propose a race of that length. "Um...ten?"

He frowned and seemed to inspect the track as well. "That sounds like a lot."

"It won't feel like a lot once you're going a hundred and fifty miles an hour."

Something that might have been the beginnings of a grin touched Nasim's lips. Bailey couldn't say for sure, because she knew that staring at his mouth would only get her into trouble. "You have raced here before?"

She shook her head. "Just watched, and helped out in the pit a couple of times. But these things go fast. Trust me."

A pause as he stared down at her. The lift at the corner of his mouth was gone, and for a second he looked deadly serious. "I do trust you, Bailey. I wish you would trust me."

Oh, hell. They certainly didn't need to get into this now. For all she knew, Nasim was just messing with her, trying to get inside her head and throw her off right as the race was about to begin. It seemed like the kind of trick a djinn would pull. Well, she wasn't about to let him get away with it.

"I trust you," she said, her tone light. "Most of the time."

He frowned and straightened up. "Good to know. I'll see you at the finish line."

After delivering that parting shot, he sauntered back to his hornet-hued car and climbed inside. A moment later, Bailey heard a few revs of the engine. Just another way for him to mess with her, or was he trying to get more of a feel for the car than what he'd gotten during his short drive over to the starting line?

Probably a little of both.

She pulled in a breath, gaze sliding toward the clock on the dash. One minute to go. How long would it take to race ten laps? Assuming an average speed of one hundred miles per hour, she figured they could get this wrapped up in about fifteen minutes, give or take. Not a very long span of time to determine the course the rest of your life might take.

Twenty seconds.

Her heart rate began to speed up, but she ignored it, kept her fingers wrapped around the steering wheel, her body braced for the acceleration soon to come. It was stuffy in here, with the warm sun beating down on her, and yet she knew better than to turn on the air conditioning. She couldn't afford even the slightest drain on the P1's engine.

Five seconds.

Was Nasim as tense as she was, or did he regard this whole arrangement as only some kind of game, a way to amuse himself for a while until something better came along? She supposed the djinn had to work pretty hard to keep themselves occupied all the long days of their lives, and so might invent some fairly novel pursuits to keep themselves from going crazy from boredom.

But that was no concern of hers.

One second.

Her foot came down on the accelerator, and even though Bailey had prepared herself for this, had known that the P1's monster of a powerplant delivered neck-snapping acceleration, she still couldn't quite believe the force that pushed her back into the driver's seat, as if some invisible giant's hand was holding her in place, keeping her from breathing. The McLaren leapt away from the starting line, moving so fast that the stands and the palm trees and everything else that surrounded her turned into a blur.

Zero to sixty in 2.1 seconds went through her mind. She seemed to recall reading that somewhere.

The only thing that wasn't a blur was Nasim's yellow and black vehicle. It was almost nose and nose with her, maybe an inch or so behind her lead. The car's tinted windows wouldn't allow her to see much of him except a vague blur of an outline, but she got the impression he was hunched slightly forward, as though willing the P1 to go faster.

Well, she wasn't going to allow that to happen.

They were already coming up on the turn, and she eased off the accelerator just slightly but not enough to require the car to downshift. This resulted in some oversteer, the rear end slipping a bit, but it wasn't enough to pull her out of her lane, and as soon as she reached the straightaway, her foot went right back down on the gas pedal.

The maneuver helped her to pull a few feet ahead of Nasim. Exactly what she'd hoped would happen, but she knew she couldn't allow herself to relax even the slightest bit. This race would be much shorter than the competitions that used to draw huge crowds to the speedway, true, and yet there was still plenty of time for her to screw up royally if she didn't pay attention.

A quick glance at the speedometer. A hundred and twenty-two miles per hour, and the next turn was coming up quickly. Once again she reduced the pressure on the gas pedal, slowing more than she had on the previous turn, since she didn't want to oversteer again, wanted to rocket out of the turn tight and fast.

That strategy proved to be a mistake, because Nasim shot past her, pulling almost a car length ahead. Bailey ground out a curse and immediately slammed her foot down on the accelerator. The P1 shot forward like it had been propelled out of a catapult, allowing her to draw almost even with him.

Better, but not good enough.

Her vehicle was already in race mode, so there

was only so much she could do to coax any additional performance from it. One very small advantage she had working for her was that she weighed a good bit less than Nasim. Was the difference enough to hand her the victory?

She had to hope so, but she knew she didn't dare take anything for granted.

On the next lap, she focused more on keeping her speed consistent, even if it meant drifting out of her lane as she took the turn. Doing so cost her less time than slowing down but being more careful about staying between the lines. In a crowded field, that might have been dangerous, could have precipitated a crash. Here, with Nasim as her only competitor, Bailey decided it was worth the risk.

The strategy seemed to work, because during the entire third and fourth laps, she was able to maintain a lead of almost a car length. Her breathing slowed a bit, and she let her death grip on the steering wheel relax ever so slightly, even though she knew better than to believe her current lead would last forever. Sure enough, as they entered the fifth lap, Nasim seemed to come from nowhere, coaxing an extra burst of speed from his vehicle, one that sent him screaming past her once they entered the straightaway.

Goddamn it.

Right then, she wished her car had nitrous so

she could obliterate the lead he'd just taken, but these P1s were bone-stock, no modifications made to them. As sanity prevailed, she realized that was probably a good thing; the McLaren was speedy enough on its own. A burst of nitrous would make this car go so fast, she was pretty sure she would never have been able to control it.

Well, she'd have to do this the old-fashioned way.

As they headed into the final turn of the fifth lap, Bailey barely slowed at all, allowing her car to drift around the curve, tires screaming, smoke billowing around her. Not even a second of hesitation, and her foot was pushing the accelerator to the floor as soon as she hit the straightaway.

In less than a second, Nasim was once again trailing her.

Yes, that was better.

Since the strategy had worked already, she employed it again on the next turn. In her rearview mirror, she could see Nasim attempting the same thing. However, she'd been "drifting" cars since she was seventeen years old, whereas the djinn probably hadn't even known such a maneuver was possible.

Now her lead was more than a car length, and she had begun to feel a lot better about the world. Yes, they still had three and a half laps to go, but so far Nasim hadn't shown any evidence of being able to close up the gap between them. Their cars were evenly matched, and so it all came down to their individual skills as drivers.

She wouldn't relax until she crossed the finish line, though.

That was a good thing, because after maintaining her lead through the seventh and eighth laps, he began to inch up on her. How exactly he was managing to do such a thing, when she couldn't see anything different about his technique, she didn't know.

Which was why you should never, ever get cocky.

They were nose and nose again as they came into the final turn. Bailey couldn't allow herself to look over at Nasim or at his bumblebee-yellow car, couldn't do anything except keep her eyes ahead and her fingers clenched on the steering wheel. By that point, her neck and shoulders had begun to ache from the strain of keeping this beast of a car from roaring out of control, but she ignored the discomfort. Almost there....

Impossibly, Nasim pulled ahead as they came out of the turn. Not by much, but he shouldn't have been able to gain any kind of a lead, not when they were both going flat out.

Or almost flat out. They'd been cruising the straightaways at a little more than 160 miles per hour, but Bailey knew the cars could do more.

Already she was driving faster than she ever had before, and yet....

Her foot pushed down on the accelerator. *165...178...184....*

The world was a blur. Nothing existed except this cockpit and the stretch of road before her. Her arms shook, but she made them hold the steering wheel steady. Just the slightest deviation at this speed, and she could send the P1 tumbling, flipping end over end until it crashed up against the wall that separated the track from the empty stands beyond.

Nasim had been able to put her back together after her last crash, but she doubted he could save her from a wreck like that, despite the McLaren's hefty roll-cage.

She didn't know why she so desperately needed to win. Would it really be that terrible to become Nasim's lover? Was it worth risking her life, just to prove she was the better driver?

Bailey wasn't sure about the first question, but she knew the answer to the second. Yes, it was worth it. If nothing else, she would have proved that a human could beat a djinn, that they weren't invincible. She could take that information to the survivors in Los Alamos, let them know never to give up hope.

Something yellow in her rearview mirror was approaching, and fast. But not fast enough.

Her night-black vehicle sailed over the finish line almost a car length ahead of Nasim's. At once she eased off the accelerator, slowing gradually, coming to a stop just before the track began to curve again. Her heart was pounding, and for the first time she was aware of the sweat trickling down her temples and trailing its way down her back, making her T-shirt stick to her under the damp weight of the leather jacket she wore.

It didn't matter, though. None of it mattered. She'd won.

Why, then, did she feel so strangely hollow?

Pushing aside her sudden surge of misgivings, she turned off the engine, patted the dash cover as a way of saying thank-you to the P1 for its astonishing performance, and then climbed out of the car. Her legs were shaking, but she made herself stand calmly where she was as Nasim pulled up next to her and got out of his own vehicle.

His face was completely blank. Right then, Bailey couldn't tell if he was angry at himself for losing, or angry at her for winning. Maybe a little of both.

For a second, he stood where he was, next to the open door of his vehicle. Then he shut that door very carefully and came around the front of Bailey's car, stopping a foot or so away from her. He extended his hand. "Good race."

She took it, feeling sort of surreal. He

squeezed her fingers for a second or two but then let go, helping to relieve her fear that he might continue to grip her hand so he could pull her toward him. "Thanks," she said, doing her best to keep her tone completely neutral. Because it had to be said, she added, "So…what now?"

Nasim crossed his arms. "I suppose it depends on how you want to handle things. I've never been to Los Alamos, but I can look it up on a map. Once I know where it is, I can take you there directly. Or you can drive, and I can follow, make sure you're safe."

The thought of showing up in Los Alamos with a vehicle of her own choosing sounded appealing at first. But, even though she wasn't exactly sure where the place was located, she knew it had to be about a thousand miles from where she stood now. That would be one long drive. Anyway, even though there were survivors living in the town, there had to be plenty of abandoned vehicles still available. Maybe not Porsches and Ferraris and McLarens, but something she could drive.

Anyway, wasn't the whole point to get away from Nasim as quickly as possible? How awkward would it be for him to ride shotgun during the course of a fifteen-hour drive? Besides, the longer they were on the road, the more likely they would be to attract unwanted attention. No, it was better to have him take her there djinn-style, or at least as close as he could get.

"You can take me," she said. "I think it would be simpler."

"Then we might as well go back to the lofts. You can pack a few things, and I can take a look at a map."

Bailey nodded. It would be good to bring some clothes and toiletries with her, just enough to fit in one small bag. Finding it hard to look at him directly, she asked, "The cars?"

"I'll send them back to the garage after we get to the lofts." For the first time, he smiled slightly, although it was a rueful one. "Don't worry—I won't leave them sitting out here."

She hadn't thought he would show these fine vehicles that kind of disrespect, but it relieved her to know he already had a plan for them. "Good."

It felt strange to step toward him, to have him put his arms around her. His T-shirt felt slightly damp beneath her fingertips, so she knew he must have perspired during the race as well. For a moment, Bailey closed her eyes, feeling the strength of his body pressed against hers, inhaling the clean scent of his sweat. Despite the disorientation of their travel, it seemed right to be held like this.

But no, it wasn't right. He was a djinn. The world had ended because of people like him.

And then it was over, and he was stepping away from her, that same fiercely blank expression on his face. Had he been fighting his attraction to her, telling himself that this was done, she had won?

Bailey couldn't know for sure, and she sure as hell wasn't going to ask.

"Go ahead and pack," he told her, then turned away.

Since there didn't seem to be anything she could say, she did as he asked, and left.

THIRTEEN

He'd lost. How could that have happened?

Nasim didn't know. He'd kept up with her, even passed her a few times. They'd seemed almost perfectly evenly matched. And then there had been that surge of power, that fierce acceleration, the one which sent her shooting ahead of him like a horse that had just been kicked.

There was no magic involved, no trick. It was only that Bailey knew cars better than he did, how to handle them, how they worked. Indeed, he'd probably only won their second race because he was more familiar with the course they'd driven. Given that same knowledge, she probably would have beaten him then as well.

Scowling, he snapped his fingers and conjured a map of New Mexico, then spread it out on the dining room table. There was Los Alamos, a small dot on a map that showed a great deal of empty space. The state did not seem terribly populated, especially when compared to California and the dense metropolis where he'd met Bailey.

Ah, God, she had felt so good in his arms. It had been one of the hardest things he'd done, letting go of her when he only wanted to pull her close and kiss her, but he'd made a promise. He'd lost the bet, and he'd lost her as well.

There was nothing he could do about that, at least nothing that was honorable. He knew of some djinn who would have shrugged aside such a bargain, would have kept Bailey for their own even though that would mean breaking their agreement. However, Nasim knew he was not such a djinn. If she was to go, so be it.

He returned his attention to the map. Los Alamos was not large, and neither was the closest town, a place called Española. It would be easy enough to find Bailey's destination in all that open land. But because Los Alamos was guarded by devices that nullified a djinn's magic, he could not get too close. He didn't know what would happen if he crossed over into the devices' field of effect while traveling outside time and space, as he and his people did, but he guessed it would not be pleasant. Because of that, he decided it would be better to appear a bit outside Los

Alamos proper, in what looked to be a trading post off one of the highways that led into town. She would have a walk of several miles, but he would stay with her until they came to the border of the safe zone. Then he would remain behind, and she could continue into Los Alamos itself, secure in the knowledge that the devices were protecting her and that she need fear no djinn attack.

It sounded like a simple enough plan. The only problem was whether he would have the strength to go through with it.

———

She didn't have much to pack—a couple of T-shirts, an extra pair of jeans, several changes of underwear. Bailey knew the black weekender bag hadn't been in her closet when she'd gotten dressed this morning, so she assumed Nasim had put it there when they'd returned to the lofts a few minutes earlier.

Everything fit well enough, even when she added her toothbrush and toothpaste, moisturizer and the rest of her toiletries. The bag wasn't heavy, and so it shouldn't slow Nasim down as he was transporting her to Los Alamos.

In a few minutes, she'd be leaving Los Angeles behind forever. She should have been happy, glad to get away, relieved to be going someplace where she would be surrounded by humans like herself.

Problem was, she didn't feel very happy. In fact, she pretty much felt like crap.

It's just nerves, she told herself. *You'll be the new kid in school, and that always feels weird.*

However, she didn't think it was nerves. Getting bumped from foster home to foster home and always going to new schools had pretty much forced her to be adaptable. She'd never had a problem meeting people, had always made sure she presented to strangers as someone entirely sure of herself, even if on the inside she might be having something close to a panic attack. Surely the survivors in Los Alamos would be happy to see another person who'd managed to stay alive all these months, so it wasn't as though she feared the reception they would give her.

Mouth pressed into a grim line, she zipped the weekender bag shut. The one thing she absolutely would not allow herself to do was consider that the dread beginning to churn in her gut had a hell of a lot more to do with the man in the loft next to hers than it did with any worry about what her new life in Los Alamos might be like.

Not a man, she thought automatically. *A djinn.*

Problem was, that argument had begun to feel pretty stale.

She lifted the bag from where it had been resting at the foot of the bed and headed for the door. No point in checking to make sure everything was picked up; she hadn't made much of a mess here in the first place, and she supposed Nasim would clear away any signs of her presence.

At least, she knew she would do the same thing if she was in his shoes.

Steeling herself, she went over to the door to his loft and knocked once. A second or two passed, and then Nasim answered her knock, his face still so fiercely expressionless, it was almost an expression itself.

"Ready?" he asked.

Right then she was pretty sure she wasn't, not really, but she had no intention of telling him that. "Yes," she replied.

He didn't invite her inside. Instead, he stepped out into the hallway and extended a hand. "Let me hold the bag," he said. "It'll be easier for you to hang on to me as we travel if you don't have that thing in the way."

No point in arguing. She gave the bag to him, then moved closer, wrapped her arms around his waist. It felt as though he'd changed his shirt; this one looked identical, a plain black crew-neck T-shirt, but it was dry, not damp with perspiration. An inconsequential detail, but at least she could focus on that and not the sensation of his muscled chest pressed against hers, or how strong his arms were.

A blink, and they were gone.

When they reappeared, they were in a place that didn't look very much like Los Alamos. Not that Bailey had any clear idea exactly what Los Alamos was supposed to look like, but she supposed she'd figured that the place where they'd built atomic bombs wouldn't be a low adobe-looking building surrounded by cottonwood trees.

"Where are we?" she asked.

"A trading post a few miles outside Los Alamos," Nasim told her. Face still blank, he extended the hand that held her bag, and she took it. "I wasn't sure how much of the surrounding countryside was shielded by the devices, so I thought it would be safer to come here. We'll walk until we get to the edge of the protected area, and then you can go on alone."

Alone. That image didn't seem very appealing, but she was the one who'd decided on this course of action. She couldn't very well back out now. "That makes sense. Which way is it?"

He pointed to a gravel lane a few feet from where they stood. "That road connects to the main highway. We'll head west from there. Come on."

Without waiting for her, he began to walk in the direction he'd indicated. Bailey followed in silence, weekender bag dangling from one hand. Maybe there was something she could have said, something she could have done to keep herself from coming to this place, but now it seemed as though the only thing she could do was follow this through to the end. At some point it would have to stop hurting, right?

The landscape was barren, forbidding. Bailey could see a single line of trees cutting across the dusty countryside. Probably following some kind of water source, a river or creek, but she didn't know enough about that sort of thing to tell for sure. Her entire life had been spent in Southern California's endless miles of tract homes and shopping malls and overcrowded streets, and what she knew about the great outdoors could fit in the palm of her hand.

But at least looking around helped to distract her a little, and kept her from brooding about the tense silence that surrounded the two of them as they walked along the deserted highway. Unlike the roads and freeways back in Los Angeles, this one was completely clear, the vehicles that had once been abandoned there either removed entirely or pushed off onto the shoulder or median. That meant Bailey and Nasim were able to walk at a brisk pace. Maybe that was a good thing. She could get this over with quickly, leave the djinn behind, move on to her new life.

They came to a place where the highway split off in a fork, one section heading up a steep hill toward Los Alamos, the other one winding away toward Española. Here, Nasim stopped abruptly, his face going white. His footsteps stumbled, and for a moment Bailey thought he was going to fall right over.

"What is it?" she asked. If he collapsed here in the middle of the road, what in the world would she be able to do for him?

He took a hasty step backward. Almost at once, his color returned, and he seemed taller somehow, although she would have thought that was impossible. "This is where the devices' effects begin. All you have to do is cross the line here, and you'll be protected."

It was almost on Bailey's lips to say that she didn't need to be protected from him, but she realized what he meant. Everything beyond this point, on that long, lonely road up into Los Alamos, was shielded by the strange devices the people in that mountain town had built. All she had to do was take a step.

Why, then, did she feel as though she was frozen in place, unable to move? Her breath caught in her throat, and she knew it wasn't because of the dry mountain air.

"Bailey?" Nasim said. His tone didn't seem

particularly concerned—more impatient than anything—as he asked, "Are you all right?"

No, she wasn't all right. She realized that now. They still stood on solid enough ground, here at the intersection of two highways with cliffs of pale stone all around them, but she might as well have been standing on a precipice for as secure as she felt right then. The world seemed to tilt around her as she finally understood.

She couldn't leave him. She couldn't turn her back, walk up that steep road, because if she did so, she'd never see him again, and the very idea of doing such a thing, taking such a final step, made harsh tears sting her eyes.

Fingers knotted around the handles of the weekender bag she held, she said, "I—I don't know if I'm all right. I just know that I can't leave you."

For a moment, he only stood there, staring at her. He probably thought she'd lost her mind. Bailey couldn't really blame him for that, because she knew that her reversal now must seem like utter craziness to someone looking in from the outside. After all, she'd spent the last few days protesting that she didn't want him, didn't want to be with him, only wanted to go so she could find her destiny with the rest of the world's survivors.

Now, though, she recognized a truth she hadn't wanted to acknowledge. It wasn't just that she reacted physically to him. There was much more to their connection than simple lust. If that were the case, she might have permitted herself to sleep with him, knowing she could walk away any time she wanted to.

Unfortunately, she realized she'd have to admit that she was in love with him.

When he spoke, his voice was harsh. Very likely, he thought she was toying with him. "What are you talking about, Bailey?"

She dropped the weekender bag on the pavement, then stepped closer to him. Although he didn't move, she reached over and twined her fingers in his. "I think—" Could she even say the words? She'd never even uttered them to Diego, and he'd been her one and only relationship that had lasted longer than a few weeks. "I think I might care for you, Nasim."

A flash in those bright blue eyes, a flicker of an impossible hope. Almost immediately, though, his mouth tightened. "So what are you saying? That this was all just a game?"

"No," she replied at once. "Nothing like that. I didn't—I guess I was trying to fool myself. I wanted to believe that I didn't care about you, because it seemed wrong to admit I had feelings for a djinn. It was only when we got here, and I realized I'd have to walk away and leave you behind, that I figured it out. I was being a clueless jerk, and I'm sorry."

Still he didn't move, and cold worry darted through her. Very likely, this was all too little, too late. Maybe once upon a time he'd wanted her, but after she'd played with his emotions, made it look as though she was going to walk out on him forever—

"You were being a jerk," Nasim said at last. However, the hard note was gone from his voice, and he almost smiled. "I think I understand why, though." He moved closer to her, his fingers tightening on hers. "You truly don't want to go to Los Alamos?"

Bailey shook her head. That was the last thing she wanted right now. The first thing—

She went up on her tiptoes, pressing her mouth to his. They kissed, tasting each other, bodies pressed together, and as the desire grew in her, she wondered why the hell she had ever tried to get away from him in the first place.

Abruptly, though, he broke away from her, a frown pulling at his straight brows. "Someone's coming."

At first, she couldn't figure out what he was talking about. Then she heard the low rumble of an engine—a big truck, probably a Ford F-250 or a Dodge Ram. Sure enough, coming down the winding highway from Los Alamos was a white vehicle with off-road lights mounted to the roofline. It was too far away for her to make out the model, but her guess that it was a large half-ton truck seemed to be correct.

"You think they saw us?"

"I don't know," Nasim replied, eyes narrowing as he gazed up at the truck. "But I don't intend to stick around to find out. Grab your bag."

Startled, Bailey bent down and picked up the weekender bag she'd dropped on the pavement. Just as she was looping it over her arm, Nasim grasped her by the waist and blinked her away.

The walls of his borrowed loft appeared around them. She let out a breath, still a little shaken from the abrupt change of scenery—or maybe that was just the aftereffects of their kiss.

"Much better," he said, and he cupped her face in his hands, fingers warm and strong against her cheeks. "I assume it's all right to kiss you again?"

"Yes, I think so," she said demurely, blood already racing at the thought of another embrace from him.

His mouth came down on hers, hard, hungry, his tongue touching hers as his hands moved from her face to take her by the shoulders, gripping her tightly as if he feared she might try to get away.

No chance of that. She wanted this, wanted

much more than this. How could she have been so stupid as to try to leave him?

Because as much as she needed him, that desire frightened her. It meant she was willing to acknowledge her connection to someone who wasn't even human, who looked like a man but was something else entirely.

As he clung to her, kissed her, she thought she might be okay with that.

Eventually, they both came up for air. Bailey stared up at Nasim, wondering if anyone had ever made her feel quite this excited, quite this alive.

No, she was pretty sure no one else had even come close.

"You want to tell me about this change of heart?" he inquired, eyebrow lifting at that ironic angle which both irritated her and made her want to push him down on the nearest couch and proceed to the main event.

"What's to tell?"

The eyebrow remained quirked. "From where I stand, just about everything."

Oh, no, she wouldn't tell him everything. Even though she now realized how much she cared for him, there were some things she needed to keep to herself. "I guess—I suppose I figured it out when it hit home that I was going to have to leave you there and head up to Los Alamos by myself. It just…it *hurt*. I didn't want to do it."

A nod, and then he pulled her to him again—not to kiss her this time, but only to hold her close, his arms wrapped around her in a fierce embrace. "I'm glad you listened to your heart."

Head pillowed against his muscled chest, Bailey could only be very, very glad as well. "I wish I'd listened earlier. I'm not so great at that sometimes."

"I hadn't noticed," Nasim remarked dryly. "So…you're going to stay with me?"

She almost replied, *For now,* but realized that was a cop-out. Even though she'd confessed her feelings to him, she still had no clear idea where all this was going. And did it matter so much? Every day she would be able to spend with him was a gift. She would be stupid to waste it.

"Yes," she said.

"Good," he said. "Because I have someplace I would like to take you."

As soon as their feet touched the patterned concrete walkway, Bailey looked around at their surroundings in some awe. "Where are we?" she asked. "It's so green."

Nasim supposed that, after spending six months hiding amongst downtown L.A.'s glass and steel canyons, the grounds at the Montelena

Winery would look especially verdant. "This is my home."

"The winery?"

"Yes."

She stepped a few paces away from him and surveyed the pond with its surround of lush lawn, the towering oaks and pine trees in the distance, the graceful willows that grew at the water's edge. "I guess I never thought it would look like this. There was San Antonio Winery in L.A., but it was in an industrial area."

He hadn't known about that particular winery. Too bad, because it might have been worth a visit. "Well, it is definitely not industrial here. Come along—let me show you the apartment."

"Apartment?"

"Yes—the chateau had a living space on the same level as the wine tasting room."

Bailey's expression turned somewhat dubious, as though she wasn't sure such an apartment would be much of an improvement over their downtown lofts. Nasim had to repress a smile, because of course he knew what awaited them.

Her mouth did drop open slightly as they made their way around a bend and the winery's main building came into view. It had been constructed to look like a true French chateau, all warm stone with old, old ivy growing on the façade. Stacks of wine barrels sat out front, adding to the old world atmosphere.

"I can't believe there was someplace like this in California," Bailey said as they went in the front entrance into the wine tasting room. He hadn't done anything to alter it, and so it still appeared as though ready for business, dusty bottles stacked on the shelves behind the long counter, the stone walls reminding visitors that they truly were inside a chateau.

"Oh, this state of yours hid many treasures," Nasim responded. "You only had to seek them out."

Her mouth pursed as she appeared to consider his comment. "Well, all right, I went to the Huntington Library on a school field trip once, but that wasn't really the same thing."

"No, because there wouldn't have been any wine. Speaking of which"—he gestured toward the bottles behind the bar—"would you like a drink?"

"That sounds like a great idea."

He smiled at her and went to fetch a bottle of petite sirah. After taking it down from the shelf and getting them a couple of glasses—and discreetly blowing the dust from each of them— he opened the wine. "You should like this," he said as he poured petite sirah into the glasses. "I would have started us with something white, but because I haven't been in residence, I'm afraid the refrigerators weren't running."

"Somehow, I'll make do," Bailey remarked, her blue eyes glinting up at him.

They should probably toast, but to what? Their suddenly reclaimed future? That she had at last come to her senses? Nasim wasn't sure she would appreciate that one. "To fast cars," he said as they clinked glasses.

"I'll definitely drink to that," she replied before taking a swallow of her wine. "Mmm... that is good. I think I could get used to this."

"I'm glad to hear it."

She came over and kissed him—not a lingering kiss like the ones they'd shared before, but a quick touch of mouth against mouth, as if she just wanted to show that she didn't regret their earlier intimacy, and wanted to reassure him that there would be more very soon.

Heat flooded through him, desire for her, but he did his best to push it aside. Time for that later. "Let me show you the apartment."

He headed toward a door that was nearly concealed within the paneling, then opened it, revealing a long hallway whose walls were lined with landscapes of the rolling Napa countryside. Beyond the hallway was a large room with tall windows that looked out on the winery entrance and the green lawns beyond.

Whoever had decorated the space had taken the winery's French inspiration seriously, for the interior reminded Nasim of the various chateaux he had visited in the Loire Valley, with their mismatched but somehow harmonious antiques and muted colors. A mellow light filled the room, and a certain tension that had occupied his body almost his entire time in Los Angeles began to quietly drift away.

"This is beautiful," Bailey said. "People actually lived here?"

"I believe the winery's owners stayed here from time to time, although it wasn't their primary residence. There is a large dining room that was used for wine club events, I believe. But it is all mine now."

"It's so different from...." She began, then seemed to stop herself. Nasim had a feeling she spoke of the group homes that had formed much of her childhood experience, and not the lofts they'd left behind in downtown Los Angeles.

"It does feel like a world apart," he agreed. "But let's go sit down, shall we?"

"Sure."

They went over to one of the sofas and sat next to each other. Even though he'd already kissed her, there was something intoxicating about being this close as she brought the glass of wine to her lips and drank, about watching the delicate muscles of her throat move as she swallowed. Something about her still seemed somewhat tense, like a bird ready to take flight at any sudden movement.

Well, he would have to make sure he did nothing to startle her.

"Do you think they were coming after us?" Bailey asked suddenly. "The people in the truck at Los Alamos, I mean."

"I don't know," Nasim replied. He had a feeling she had brought up the subject simply because it was a somewhat neutral topic, nothing as fraught as having to discuss the sudden change in their relationship. "It's possible they had some kind of perimeter surveillance set up. We djinn don't know much about what's going on in that town, obviously, because we can't get close enough to see anything for ourselves."

"But they'll know you were a djinn because of the way you disappeared."

"Probably."

She was silent for a moment, sipping at her wine, her gaze fixed on the view outside the tall windows, although Nasim guessed she was thinking of someplace much farther away than the pond and the trees that surrounded it. "And if I'd hesitated for much longer—"

"But you didn't," Nasim cut in. The last thing he wanted was her to get lost in self-recriminations for something that had a happy outcome after all. "You looked into your heart and saw the truth there. What else did you need?"

Her eyes met his. She set her glass down on the stone coffee table before them and said simply, "Nothing. Because I had you."

The only logical response was to put down his wine and take her in his arms. She kissed him, her body warm and alive, her lips tasting of wine, and relief rushed over him. They were here, and she was his, and everything was well with the world.

FOURTEEN

THIS PLACE WAS LIKE SOMETHING OUT OF A dream, or at least a movie or some glossy lifestyle magazine, the kind that Bailey would never have dreamed of picking up because she knew she couldn't afford anything in it. After a pretty heavy make-out session on the couch—which she thought might turn into something more, but didn't—Nasim took her by the hand and showed her the rest of the apartment. There were two bedrooms, both decorated with the same interesting antiques and muted shades of cream and green and rose, a huge bathroom with marble countertops, walls, and floors, and the dining room he had mentioned earlier, one with a table big enough to seat twenty people.

The larger of the two bedrooms had a walk-in closet, and Bailey supposed she shouldn't have been surprised to find her clothes already hanging in there, along with a few additions she was pretty sure she'd never seen before. One was a halter dress in a deep royal blue, the sort of thing she might have noticed on the rack but would never have thought to bring home. It was way too fancy for her everyday life, but not skimpy enough for her modeling gigs at the racetrack.

"Would you wear it to dinner tonight?" Nasim asked as she turned away from the dress and back toward him.

"Dressing for dinner?" she responded, knowing her tone was too flip but not sure what she should do about it. "How classy."

He didn't appear offended. A small smile playing around his lips, he said, "I thought the venue deserved something more than a T-shirt and jeans."

Well, she wouldn't argue with him about that. Already she felt intimidated by the elegance of the place, which was so far outside her experience, she might as well be at Buckingham Palace instead of merely a winery in Northern California. Besides, she actually did like dressing up, even though she hardly ever got a chance to do it—and would never have admitted such a thing in a million years.

"I suppose it does. It's going to feel weird

eating at that table with all those empty chairs, though."

Nasim's mouth quirked further. "Oh, I have something better in mind than that."

And it turned out he did. Once she'd changed —and he'd traded his own jeans and T-shirt for djinn clothing, an open robe of sky-blue silk almost the color of his eyes, with trousers in a darker shade of the same blue and wide silver cuffs on both his wrists—he guided her out of the winery building and along the pathway that bordered the pond, clearly intent on a particular destination. That turned out to be a pagoda, of all things, perched on its own little island a ways out from the shore of the pond. They reached the pagoda by traversing a small bridge of red-painted wood, with Bailey's high heels clacking the whole way. Thank God she'd learned to walk in those things during her modeling days, although they weren't exactly her footwear of choice for an outdoor expedition.

However, once they'd sat down at the small table placed in the center of the pagoda, already set with a fine white cloth and fancy china and real crystal wine goblets, she was able to relax a little, take in the beauty of their surroundings. The early evening light shimmered on the water, and a few clouds drifting above the far-off hills reflected sunset colors of copper and coral.

It was hard to believe that only a little more than six hours earlier, she'd been piloting a McLaren P1 around the Auto Club Speedway track. Already, that race—and her months of being hunted in downtown L.A.—was starting to feel like something that had happened in a dream.

"The elders must really like you, to have given you a place like this," she commented as Nasim uncorked a bottle of chardonnay and poured some for the two of them.

"I'm not sure it was a matter of 'liking' me," he replied as he sat down across from her. "To be perfectly honest, none of us have actually been able to figure out why they gifted lands as they did. I suppose there must have been some sort of rhyme or reason to it, even if it eludes the rest of us djinn."

"Where do the elders live?"

Nasim stared at her for a moment, as if realizing he'd never wondered the same thing himself, then shook his head. "I don't think any of us know. At least, I do not. They had their palace in the otherworld—"

"The world where you djinn used to live."

"Yes," he said, acknowledging her interruption before continuing. "They had a fine palace there, but of course they must come to Earth at last, the same as the rest of us. I have heard nothing of where they plan to settle here, however. Possibly, they don't want the rest of us djinn to know. They come and go as they please, and so I think it's plausible to believe that they would rather us not have any idea where their own sanctuary is located."

"They live together?" Bailey asked, intrigued. "How many of them are there?"

"Three. Ibram and Istar and Idris."

"Are they brothers and sister?"

"No." Nasim lifted his glass of chardonnay and sipped at it.

A moment later, a pair of salads materialized in front of them. Bailey jumped a little at the sudden appearance of their first course, but shrugged. Sooner or later she'd get used to this sort of thing. "What, do the elders have some sort of djinn *ménage à trois* going on?"

Her companion appeared to choke a little on the mouthful of chardonnay he'd just swallowed. Recovering himself, he replied, "No, I don't think so. That is, I've heard rumors that Ibram and Istar have some kind of intimate relationship, but of course they would never deign to confirm such a thing. Gossiping about the elders is not condoned."

"Sorry," Bailey said, although she really wasn't all that sorry. It was hard for her to wrap her head around the concept of these elders, whose word seemed to be law, but who also seemed to be MIA a good deal of the time. "When you said they all lived together in the same palace, I just kind of assumed something else was going on."

Nasim's lips quirked. "It was a very large palace. They probably could have gone a week without seeing one another, if they so chose."

"Ah." She picked up her fork and took a bite of salad. Just like everything else Nasim had provided for her to eat so far, it was delicious, romaine and field greens with some kind of balsamic dressing and tiny grape tomatoes. Normally, she wouldn't have said she was much of a salad person, but it had been so long since she'd eaten anything like it, the simple combination tasted absolutely heavenly. After she was done chewing, she said, "But you don't have to worry about the elders anymore, right? I mean, now that you're back where they told you to live."

Something about that comment apparently got to Nasim, because he frowned as he reached for his glass of chardonnay. "Well, about that...."

A twinge of alarm made her tense, but she forced herself to sit calmly, watching him. "Is there something you're not telling me, Nasim?"

His chest rose and fell as he took a breath. "Actually, there is. It's good for me to be back on the lands I was given, but I should not have brought you here with me."

"Why not?" That feeling of alarm was intensifying. It seemed like the best remedy right then was to take a steadying swallow of wine. Yes, that helped…a little.

"Because it is not allowed for a djinn and a human to be together like this."

"Like what?" she asked, then added with a curl of her lip, "I mean, we haven't even knocked boots yet." He lifted an eyebrow, and then seemed to nod, as if he'd just grasped the meaning of the human expression. "Besides, you said djinn and humans have gotten together in the past."

"Yes, but that was the past. Things are different now." He drank some of his wine and replaced his glass on the tabletop. "The only way such relationships are allowed is if the djinn takes the human as his—or her—Chosen, a partner for eternity."

Partner for eternity? Nasim had mentioned something about that after the two of them had encountered the djinn woman Fatima and her Chosen up on Mulholland Drive, but he hadn't gone into much detail about how all that was supposed to work. Bailey sat up straight in her chair, for the first time feeling a little chilly in the revealing cocktail dress she wore. A cool breeze moved across the lake, touching her shoulders and bare arms, making her shiver slightly.

Or maybe that shiver had nothing to do with the temperature at all.

"Explain that to me. How can a human be a djinn's partner for eternity when djinn live so much longer than we do?"

Nasim's fingers toyed with the stem of his wine glass. "Because when a djinn makes a human his Chosen, he lends some of his magic to her—those who are Chosen will never age, never become ill, will heal nearly as quickly as we do."

Eternal youth and health in exchange for being tied to a single djinn for eternity. That sounded like a pretty decent bargain, although Bailey found it hard to believe that those couples wouldn't start to get tired of each other after a century or two of being saddled with one another. After all, while she cared for Nasim, was only too ready to make their relationship more physical, she didn't think she could handle spending centuries with him. And if she felt that way, surely he must feel the same about her.

It was strange to contemplate, but she'd seen one of these couples already, in Fatima and her Chosen. And she'd made a comment about Bailey and Nasim coming to join their community in Bel-Air. She was actually surprised that he'd taken the risk of having a race that would bring them so close to the suburb where all those djinn and their humans lived, but maybe he hadn't.

"So you're saying that if the elders find out I'm

here with you, then they'll…what? Punish you somehow?"

Nasim shook his head. "Not exactly. Or rather, they'll tell me to either make you my Chosen or send you back to Los Angeles."

Presumably without his protection, meaning she would be prey all over again. It wouldn't be the end of the world—she'd already survived that ordeal and could do so again if necessary—but she had to admit to herself that going back to that hunted lifestyle would be like falling back into a nightmare she'd thought she'd escaped.

Even worse was the prospect of being alone again, being separated from Nasim…although she wasn't sure if she wanted to acknowledge that particular point just yet.

Crossing her arms, she settled back against her chair, felt the narrow cross-slats press into her skin. For just a second, she shivered. Yes, it was beautiful out here, but she suddenly felt as exposed as though she had a target painted on her back. Maybe it would have been better to eat dinner inside, where they would be away from prying eyes.

"This upsets you," Nasim said quietly.

"No," she said at once. "I'm not upset. I mean, I like you a lot, Nasim, but I'm not sure I want to spend an eternity with you. Or anyone else," she added hastily, in case he got the wrong idea. "I never saw myself as the settling-down type."

He didn't reply immediately, although she could see something relax about the set of his shoulders. Clearly, he hadn't been any more excited about being tied down for, well, forever than she was. "I'm glad you're not angry with me, but I also don't want to contemplate what would happen if the elders did send you back to L.A."

"I'd survive," she said with a shrug. "I did it for seven months. Or really," she continued as a thought struck her, "why would I even have to go to L.A., as long as I wasn't shacked up here with you? If you took me to Los Alamos, I'd be safe, and you'd also be doing what the elders told you to do. Win-win."

"I suppose so," Nasim allowed, although he didn't look all that enthused by her idea. With a lift at one corner of his mouth, he added, "I had intended this as a romantic dinner. I did not think we would end up discussing how this… idyll…would end."

"It can still be romantic," Bailey said. "I didn't think you brought me here so you could put a ring on my finger and we could shack up on a formal basis. I just…wanted to be with you."

This reassurance made him give her a relieved smile. "And I wanted to be with you. I'm glad we can talk like this, that there aren't any secrets between us."

She was glad of it, too. She'd always been the kind of person who would rather hear the worst and get it over with. And what Nasim had just told her—it really wasn't that bad. She'd never expected anything except a fun few weeks or months with him. They could enjoy one another and go on their separate ways once the excitement started to fade.

But if that was really the case, why did it feel so hard to fix a smile on her lips as she looked across the table at him?

Nasim was glad to see how calmly Bailey had taken the news about Chosen and djinn, how she technically shouldn't even be here with him. Although he knew her to be tough, not easily moved, he'd expected her to be at least somewhat angry that he'd concealed such an important fact. However, it seemed that she didn't mind all that much one way or another, because she'd never expected her time with him to be anything more than a fling. Oh, he knew she cared for him, or she would never have turned back to be with him as they stood on the highway in Los Alamos. Being a practical soul, though, she'd also recognized that they had very little to tie them together, except their obvious physical attraction…and perhaps a love of fast cars.

After they had finished eating their salad, they moved on to a course of veal piccata and parmesan risotto, accompanied by grilled asparagus. More wine with the veal, this time a bottle of dry rosé from the estate's vineyards. They left the topics of Chosen and elders aside, talking instead about their race that morning, and possible opportunities for driving here in Napa. Nasim had spent enough time here that he knew there were some lovely drives around the countryside— not, perhaps, suited for racing, but definitely something to be experienced in a convertible with the warm wind blowing through one's hair.

"Then let's do that tomorrow," Bailey said. She seemed more relaxed now, although possibly that was only because of all the wine she'd drunk. "To go for a drive with the top down, and not have to worry about djinn dive-bombing you? It sounds just about perfect to me."

"No, there will be no need to worry about djinn," he agreed. "These lands are empty. My nearest neighbor is at least fifty miles away."

"Awesome." She took a sip of rosé, followed by a bite of veal. "You know, this is the first time in my life I've had veal."

"Do you like it?" Nasim asked, wondering

whether he should have selected something different for their meal. "I know some mortals did not believe in eating veal, but—"

"Oh, it's not like I'm some kind of vegan or anything," Bailey cut in. "It's just that veal is expensive, you know? I was always a burgers and pizza kind of girl…well, when I wasn't trying to survive on Top Ramen while waiting for the next check from the county to show up."

He hated the thought of the troubles she'd endured, the privations she'd suffered. More than anything, he wanted to make sure she would never experience anything like that ever again. Voice gentle, he asked, "It was very difficult for you, wasn't it?"

She shrugged. "It wasn't fun. But then, I knew other people who had it worse than me. Everything's relative."

He supposed she was right, and yet he still didn't like to think of the privations she'd suffered growing up, the poverty that seemed to have followed her even into adulthood. In fact, it appeared the only lucky break she'd ever gotten was being immune to the Heat, and he wondered if she even looked on that singular quality as a benefit. Perhaps those who had died had the easier time of it, rather than having to evade the reavers, to continue in a world that no longer had any place for them.

No, he could not believe that. Certainly he did not want to think of Bailey succumbing to the deadly fever, all her vibrancy and beauty reduced to a small pile of gray ash. She had had her struggles, but she had come out on the other side of them, and he knew he would do whatever he must to make sure she remained safe.

"Still…." he began, and she smiled a little, even as she shook her head.

"Ancient history, Nasim. That was back then. The world's a different place now. *I'm* different now."

"Are you?" he asked, genuinely curious. "It seems you were a survivor then, just as you're a survivor now."

The question seemed to take her aback. He could tell she was slightly tipsy; her pupils were just a bit dilated, and she seemed far more relaxed than usual. Despite all that, he knew her reflexes and her mind were still hers, if perhaps slightly blurred.

"Maybe," she said after a long pause. "I guess I never thought about it that way. But I'm not sure the old Bailey would have come here with you."

"Why not?"

"Because she wouldn't have trusted you. Part of me thinks I'm stupid for trusting you, even now." Her head tilted to one side as she regarded him carefully. "But you kept up your side of the bargain. I knew you didn't have to. You're a djinn —you could have said no, said you were going to do whatever you wanted with me. You didn't, though. You stuck with our agreement."

"I never considered doing otherwise."

"I know. And that's why I'm here. Because that's the way you are. You're…honorable."

No doubt the elders would have a different opinion on that topic, would think he had acted dishonorably by bringing Bailey here when he knew doing so was against the rules they'd set down. However, he wasn't trying to impress the elders. Bailey knew what was in his heart, and that was the important thing. "I'm glad you think so," Nasim said quietly.

Her blue eyes glinted at him. Full night had fallen, and the pagoda was illuminated by a bowl of floating candles sitting in the center of the table, as well as little white lights that traced the borders of the roof. The lighting lent warmth to her fair skin and pale hair, made her eyes turn almost green.

"I do think so," she responded. "I also think I'm done eating. What about you?"

"No dessert?" he asked, more for her benefit than his. He'd never cared much for sweets.

The corners of her mouth turned up in a wicked smile. "You're all the dessert I want, Nasim."

Well, then.

He stood up, and she rose from her seat as well. It seemed silly to pick their way through the dark gardens while she teetered on those high heels, and so he pulled her against him, blinked them back to the apartment at the chateau.

To the bedroom, actually. As its walls materialized around them, she sent him another one of those impish grins. "Good thing I already knew you were a 'cut to the chase' type."

"Aren't you?" he countered.

"Obviously."

That seemed like enough small talk. He already held her, so it was the easiest thing in the world to pull her closer, slam his mouth down on hers. Rather than even attempt to play coy, she ground herself against him, let him taste the wine on her lips. His fingers caught in her loose hair, which fell around her bare shoulders like skeins of golden silk.

They had kissed before, but he could tell she knew this time it was different, that this time they had no reason to stop. He'd held off when they'd embraced on the couch earlier in the day, simply because he'd already had an evening envisioned for them, and he didn't want to compromise the experience by taking her on the sofa like some inexperienced youth who couldn't exercise enough self-control to wait for better things.

Well, no need to wait any longer.

His fingers found the knot of fabric at the back of her neck that held her dress in place. He tugged on it, loosening it so the bodice of her cocktail gown slipped down her waist.

A small gasp escaped her lips, but she didn't try to pull away. No, she continued to kiss him, her mouth hungry, needy, as his hands closed on the perfection of her bare breasts. The skin beneath his fingertips was soft, smooth, while her nipples grew hard at his touch.

As he bent down to take one in his mouth, however, she murmured, "Let me get these damn shoes off."

Chuckling a little, he straightened, then watched as she bent down to unfasten the ankle straps of the high-heeled sandals she wore. First one was kicked off, then the other—and then she gave a little shrug and reached back to unzip her dress so she could remove it as well.

She stood in front of him in only a pair of plain white panties. The eyes that met his were almost defiant, as if challenging him to find something wrong with her, something to prove she could never measure up to a djinn woman.

Nasim could find nothing, because she was perfection, from those long legs to her slender waist to her high, full breasts. As he began to move toward her, however, she held up a hand.

"Not so fast," she said. "I've showed you mine—now I get to see yours."

All he could do was grin at her. "If you insist."

Off came the long silk robe, the boots, the silver wrist cuffs. At last he loosened the drawstring of his pants, thinking he could do her one better…for of course djinn men did not wear any kind of undergarments beneath their loose, silky trousers.

Bailey's big blue eyes widened. "Sneaky."

She came to him and took him in her hand, stroking slowly up and down his length. Ah, God, this was what he'd been dreaming of, that she would be as bold when intimate as she was at all other times.

Apparently so, because she continued to stroke his shaft with one hand, while the other moved lower, trailing over his skin in a whisper of a touch, fingernails making a frisson of pleasure move down his spine. The hardest part would be containing himself until he was ready to bury himself in her.

In fact—

Without speaking, he pulled away from her slightly, enough so he could gather her up from the floor and throw her down on the bed. A shocked splutter was her response—one that turned into another gasp as he grasped hold of her panties and tossed them aside.

There she was, ready for him. He trailed a line of kisses along the inside of one thigh, then the other, as she shivered in his grasp. At last he tasted her, all her sweetness and her heat, burying his face in her womanhood.

She cried out loud then, a guttural sound that echoed off the high ceiling, her fingers clenched in his hair. And he felt it when the climax moved through her, shivers and shudders taking hold of her body until she could only fall back against the pillows, panting.

However, this was no time to rest.

He took her by her hips, pushed her down on her hands and knees. Part of him wondered whether she would protest, would rather have their first encounter face to face, so to speak. But as soon as he began to push into her, to feel all her sweet wetness surround him, she gasped, "Yes, Nasim. God, *yes.*"

And he pushed deeper, sensing how ready was, how much she had needed this. He held onto her hips as they found their rhythm, moving faster, harder. Then he could feel the climax rising in him, thrills of ecstasy moving all through his body, pulling him toward the precipice, closer, closer....

He groaned, and let the orgasm take him. Bailey shuddered as well, peaking just a few seconds after him, her body clenching on his shaft. So…damn…good.

For a moment, he was able to hold on to her, to hold steady as the last of the climax rippled through her. At last, though, he collapsed onto the bed, while she did as well, long pale hair spreading out over the pillow. She moved closer to him, and he slipped his arm under her so he could pull her close, so they could share in the afterglow together. Her forehead was faintly sheened with perspiration, and he thought he had never seen anyone so beautiful in all his life.

Her lips parted. For a second, he wondered if she was going to make some kind of quip about his performance, just to ease the tension.

But then she smiled and said softly, "Thank you," and he pulled her even more tightly against his body.

God help him, but he thought he might just be in love with her.

FIFTEEN

BAILEY WOKE UP AND BEGAN TO STRETCH… then froze, realizing just where she was. The damask curtains on the tall windows blocked most of the morning sun, but it was still bright enough for her to take stock of her surroundings.

Nasim's bedroom…and Nasim right there in bed next to her, apparently still asleep. His shoulder-length hair was sticking out all over the pillow, and his fine jaw and chin were faintly stubbled with hair. His eyes were closed tight, and his chest rose and fell with deep, regular breaths.

As for herself, she was wide awake…and pleasantly sore in all the places that indicated she'd just had a wild night of sex. That first time had been rough, almost primal; she didn't know how Nasim had guessed that doggy-style was her favorite position, but he'd pushed her down and taken her as if she'd beamed that image right into his mind. Later, after they'd rested and held one another, she used her lips and tongue to get him ready again, then rode him like a horse she wanted to tame. They'd collapsed into sleep after that, but had woken up in the middle of the night, both of them as horny as though they hadn't just had sex twice already. That time, they did it lying on their sides, slowly, almost dreamily, and then had fallen asleep almost immediately afterward.

Moving slowly, she slid out from under the covers and went over to the bathroom, then slipped in and quietly closed the door behind her. Once her business was attended to, she washed her hands and face, and ran her fingers through her tangled hair, doing her best to smooth it. In the mirror, her reflection seemed just about like one that belonged to a woman who'd had a wild night—mouth looking swollen and rosy from all the kissing, faint shadows under her eyes. Her neck bore a few marks that would have announced to the world exactly what she and Nasim had been up to...if anyone had been around to see them.

Luckily, there was a heavy white terrycloth bathrobe hanging from a hook on the back of the door. Bailey put it on and tied the sash around herself, feeling a bit better now that she wasn't wandering around naked. It was fine for Nasim to see her in all her boob-heaving glory when they were about to get down and dirty, but she would prefer to not to have to roam around the house in her birthday suit.

It helped to think about these practicalities, because that way she didn't have to dwell on what had passed between them the night before. Of course she'd wanted to have sex with him, but there was sex, and there was *sex*. What they'd shared hadn't been some meaningless gymnastics. When she'd looked over at him as he lay asleep just a moment before, she'd experienced a rush of tenderness unlike anything she'd ever felt before. Yes, she'd had to acknowledge to herself that she had feelings for this man—this djinn—but what she'd just experienced was different, and more than a little frightening. How could she allow herself to feel that way and still be able to leave once they'd decided their little fling was over?

Bailey didn't know. Luckily, she was saved from any further self-examination by Nasim rolling over onto his back, then leveraging himself up to a sitting position.

"When did you wake up?" he asked, reaching up with one hand to push his tousled hair off his forehead.

"Just now," she replied, then came over to the bed so she could sit down on the edge next to him. "I needed to use the bathroom."

"I'm surprised you didn't wake me."

"You looked pretty sacked out."

One eyebrow lifted. "'Sacked out'?"

"Tired."

"I suppose I was, but even so, I don't usually sleep that heavily."

Grinning, she poked him in the arm. "Guess I wore you out."

He didn't take any offense, instead smiled back at her. "Yes, I suppose you did." As if to prove her point, he gave a jaw-cracking yawn. "I think it's time for some coffee."

Coffee sounded divine. She had a feeling that he'd also come up with something awesome for breakfast, too, because that appeared to be what djinn did. They snapped their fingers and summoned their food, saving their time for more important things.

She'd already taken the bathrobe, but of course that didn't mean much. This time, Bailey didn't even see Nasim snap his fingers, but when he slid out of bed, he was wearing a pair of sweatpants that she was pretty sure hadn't been there a minute ago.

They wandered into the kitchen, where a pair of mugs filled with coffee waited for them. "Do you want cream or sugar or anything else?" he asked as he handed one of the mugs to her.

"Vanilla creamer, if you can get me some," she

replied. Normally she would take her coffee black, but from time to time she got a little more frilly with it. The creamer was an indulgence, but what the hell. She might as well celebrate her newfound intimacy with Nasim and go for it.

The words had barely left her mouth before a little container of the creamer she'd requested appeared on the countertop. "Is that the right kind?"

"Yep. Thanks." Bailey picked up the creamer, unscrewed the top, and poured some into her mug. Waiting on the countertop was a spoon, and she took that and stirred the creamer into the coffee, making sure everything was mixed well.

Her first sip was just as heavenly as she'd hoped. A certain not-unpleasant morning-after weariness had weighted her limbs, but as soon as the caffeine began coursing through her bloodstream, she began to feel more alert. Nasim sipped at his own coffee, which appeared undoctored.

Well, he seemed like the kind of person who would drink it black.

"What trouble are we going to get into today?" she asked after another sip.

His blue eyes glinted, sparkling under the halogen lighting overhead. "What, we didn't get into enough trouble last night?"

A certain heat already gathering between her legs told her she'd be up for another round, no problem. However, that wasn't really what she'd had in mind when she asked her question. "I'm not sure," she replied. "I might be up for a rematch."

He chuckled. "I'll bear that in mind. Otherwise, I need to take a look at the vines, see how everything is doing. It looks as though there was some rain here a few nights ago, which is good. But I should still see how the vineyard fared with me being gone for more than a week."

Gone because of her—or at least, gone because he'd traveled to Los Angeles in search of some sport. He couldn't have known how that little venture was going to turn out, though.

"I can do that with you," she said. "Although I'm not sure what I'd be looking for."

"Mostly you can keep me company. It shouldn't take too long—I'm not going to walk every inch of the place. But checking in on a few different varieties should tell me if any of them need some particular attention."

She drank some more coffee. "And after that?"

"I thought we'd go for a drive, find a place to have a late lunch. Maybe a picnic. Sound good?"

Picnics had never been high on her list of leisure-time activities, but then again, Bailey hadn't exactly had much opportunity for doing that sort of thing. The countryside around her looked beautiful, and she was sure Nasim would pack them something fun for lunch.

"And a bottle of wine?" she asked. Wine seemed like the sort of thing you'd take for that kind of outing, even if she'd always been more of a beer or cocktails kind of girl.

He grinned. "Naturally. You can't have a picnic in wine country without having some wine, can you?"

"Absolutely not."

"Then it's a plan."

That particular matter settled, they went out to a little breakfast nook area, where they sat at the round table there and Nasim conjured an amazing breakfast for them, one with eggs and bacon and blueberry muffins, the kind of food Bailey hadn't eaten for longer than she could recall. Even before the Heat turned the world upside down, she hadn't been the type to go out for breakfast—it just wasn't in her budget—and she sure as hell wouldn't have gone to the effort of making all this stuff at home for herself.

But it was no effort at all for Nasim, and she was starving after the exertions of the night before. She consumed a heaping plate of eggs, four pieces of bacon, and two muffins before she began to feel the slightest bit full. Good thing she was going to be walking the vineyards later this morning, or she might have worried about the amount of calories she had just eaten.

After breakfast, they both showered—separately, because after all that food, Bailey wasn't sure she wanted to participate in the kind of contortions that shower sex required. Nasim didn't seem all that disappointed, luckily; maybe he was a little worn-out, too. Or maybe he just would prefer a more leisurely lovemaking session once they were both up to it again.

Either way, it felt great to shower and wash off the sweat and the stress of the day before, and to feel the hot water pounding away at her tired muscles. There must have been another bathroom in the apartment, because Nasim reappeared just as she was getting dressed, his hair wet, a towel wrapped around his waist.

In the bright morning light, she was better able to see the amazing contours of his body, the flat stomach ridged with muscle, the breadth of his shoulders and chest. It still didn't feel quite real that she'd shared a bed with someone who looked like that, who was so unbelievably perfect in appearance.

Perfect in a lot of ways, actually. Bailey would never have said that she slept around a lot, but she wasn't exactly inexperienced, either. And she'd never been with anyone who could make her come like Nasim.

He shot her a mischievous glance as he removed the towel from around his waist. She looked at him in all his glory, and grinned.

"You're going to make me regret showering so soon."

Almost as soon as she spoke, though, he was covered up again, this time in jeans and a dark wine-colored T-shirt. "No, it's better to wait. We have things to do, after all."

Bailey almost said that she wanted to do *him,* then decided it was better just to shrug. No doubt she'd be jumping his bones as soon as they got home this evening.

Or maybe they could end their picnic with a little outdoor lovemaking. In the past, she hadn't been that big a fan, because the places the guys she'd dated had wanted to have sex outside were way too exposed—public parks, for the most part. But there certainly wasn't anyone around here to catch them at it.

Yes, that idea definitely had some merit.

Now that they were both showered and dressed, they headed out to the vineyards. Bailey was a little surprised that Nasim didn't just blink them there, but it seemed as though he wanted to do this the old-fashioned way, wanted to refamiliarize himself with his land.

She couldn't blame him for that. The sun was warm and bright overhead, the breeze fresh but not too wild, just enough to ruffle their hair and keep them from getting too hot as they hiked their way to the closest group of vines, which Nasim had said were chardonnay grapes.

This early in the season, there wasn't any fruit yet, just lush green leaves and tiny constellations of white flowers that seemed to glow from within the shadow of the vines' protective foliage. Nasim bent close to several of the vines, running a caressing hand over the leaves, but being careful not to touch the flowers.

"They look good," he said. "I can't see any signs of insect damage, or of fungus."

"Is that usually a problem?" Bailey asked. Maybe it was a stupid one. She didn't know the first thing about growing grapes—or anything else, for that matter.

"It can be, if there's too much rain. But I think there's been just enough to keep things watered without making it too damp."

"Ah." She paused for a moment, watching as he moved farther down the row, inspecting a different plant. "Nasim, do you really know how to make wine?"

The question appeared to amuse him, because he turned back toward her, a smile pulling at his lips. "Not really," he admitted. "I suppose I thought I'd figure it out somehow. But it turns out I don't need to puzzle my way through it, because when I was going over the property, I found all the winemaker's notes in a binder in the office here. I don't know why he didn't keep that information in a computer, but it's definitely better that it was written down on paper. We djinn have many powers, but hacking someone's passwords isn't among them."

That made some sense, although his admission surprised Bailey a little. She would have thought djinn would find it easy to break into a computer —but then, why would they? A few comments Nasim had made seemed to indicate that djinn didn't have much interest in human technology, except when it came to fast cars, and maybe planes and boats as well. But they certainly didn't seem to need computers.

For a moment she didn't reply, only looked past this particular field to the others that surrounded the chateau. As far as she could tell, it was all vines almost as far as the eye could see. "It seems like a lot to handle for one person—even if that person is a djinn."

"I'll manage. Or rather," he added, still smiling at her, "we'll manage. I can work very fast when I need to."

"I suppose so," she replied, not bothering to hide her skepticism. It was possible Nasim could turn into some kind of supercharged djinn grape-picker, but it wasn't as though she could manage the same thing.

Anyway, she thought, *there's a good chance you won't even be here by the time harvest rolls around. That's got to be at least four months from now, maybe more.*

She found she didn't want to think about that so much. It could have just been the afterglow of the previous night's lovemaking, but she found it hard to imagine a world without Nasim in it.

"It'll be fine," he said. "Come—let's take a look at the petite sirah."

And she followed him out of this field and over to the next, and wondered if she would ever have the strength to leave when the time came.

Bailey seemed somewhat subdued, but Nasim wondered if she was still tired from their activities of the night before. Or possibly the physical reality of all these vines had proved to be more overwhelming than he'd thought.

Whatever the case, she perked up when they were done walking the fields and headed back to the chateau, to the garage tucked away out back. Inside was a gleaming red convertible, one he'd thought would be perfect for their afternoon ride.

"It's gorgeous," Bailey said, leaning down to

inspect the badging. "I didn't even know Fiat had started making convertibles again."

"They were fairly new, I think," Nasim replied. No, this car he'd chosen didn't have the brute strength of any of the vehicles they'd driven for their races, but he preferred it that way. This wasn't an afternoon of racing, but a leisurely drive through the countryside, and the Fiat Spider's lines seemed perfect for that.

She straightened and looked over at him, one eyebrow raised slightly. "Can I drive?"

"Of course." He pulled the key fob from his pocket and handed it to her. "As long as you don't mind if I drive on the way back."

"It's a deal."

They both climbed in. The top was already down, so there was little to do to prepare for their drive—although he did conjure a pair of sunglasses and a silk scarf patterned in shades of red and black and tan for Bailey to cover her head and keep her hair from getting too tangled.

She took the items with a straight face, although he could see how her lips quirked a little at the sight of the scarf. Still, she set the sunglasses on her nose without comment and then expertly tied the scarf over her hair, making a little knot at the back to hold it in place. "I like how you coordinated the scarf with the car—and my shirt," she said as she pushed the button to start the ignition.

"Would you have gotten a green car if I was wearing green?"

"Naturally," he said, refusing to be teased. "If you pull down the lane that leads out of the winery and then turn left, we'll come to a country highway that goes through some beautiful country —and twists and turns a good bit."

"Sounds perfect." Bailey reversed out of the garage, then followed his directions, taking them out to the road that connected the winery to the highway. Once there, she increased their speed, but not too much, just enough to get a feel for the car and what it could do.

Nasim watched her drive, rather than paying attention to the landscape around him. This part of the world was lovely, of course, with its rolling hills that alternated stands of oak with the straight, geometric patterns of the various vineyards, but it couldn't compare to the woman who expertly piloted their convertible along the narrow two-lane road, a small smile touching her mouth as she took them around the first curve and then straightened out again, gaining speed.

"Well, it's no Porsche 911, but I think I like it," she remarked. "It's a good touring car."

"Which is exactly why I chose it. By the way, in about five miles, we'll come to a private lane. You'll want to turn off there."

"Our picnic spot?"

"Yes."

She nodded and kept driving, sometimes speeding up, sometimes slowing to take another curve, all the while putting the car through its paces. Nasim let himself rest against the seat back, enjoying the feel of the wind blowing through his loose hair, watching as sometimes the sky above was nearly hidden by the trees stretching overhead, concealing them in a canopy of green.

In fact, he was so lost in his enjoyment of the ride that he nearly didn't rouse himself in time to call out their turnoff. "Here," he told Bailey, and she slowed immediately and took a hard right, slowing again when she realized their route took them along a gravel lane. It twisted and turned for a while, eventually ending at a handsome property with a low, sprawling house and several outbuildings.

Bailey pulled up in front of one of those, put the car in park, then sent Nasim a quizzical glance from behind her sunglasses. "A house?" she asked. "I thought we were going on a picnic."

"We are," he replied, unperturbed. "The house is incidental. We're here because of the lake."

He pointed toward the body of water in question, which was partially blocked by the house. However, once they got out of the car and followed the path, they would be able to see the lake very clearly—as well as the little grove of oak trees that would serve as the setting for their picnic.

"Okay," Bailey said. "Lead on, I guess."

They both climbed out of the low-slung convertible. Then Nasim took the lead, walking along the flagstone path, ignoring the point where it branched off toward the large patio off the back of the house. Bailey was right behind him, looking from side to side.

"This seems like a pretty nice spread," she commented. "I wonder why the elders put you in the winery instead of out here."

"I don't know," he replied, and truly, he didn't. This house was large and well-appointed; he knew that, because he'd explored it after stumbling upon the property while exploring the countryside one day. Perhaps he had been ensconced at the winery so that he might become its caretaker— and make sure the djinn community never ran out of wine. Why that particular winery, he had no idea, although he supposed the presence of the chateau building had something to do with it.

Bailey grinned. "Those mysterious elders."

All Nasim could do was shrug. Their motives often were mysterious, which was why he tried not to waste too much time puzzling over them.

At any rate, it wasn't something to worry about now, not when their destination was almost upon them. There was the little grove of trees, and there was the blanket he'd wanted spread upon the grass, and the wicker picnic basket waiting for them.

"Well, that's convenient," she said.

"It seemed simpler than carrying it all the way from the car."

"True."

They both went to settle themselves on the blanket, and then Nasim busied himself with pulling out all the food he thought would make a good picnic lunch—a tray of sliced sausage and prosciutto, another tray of various cheeses, grapes, a long loaf of crusty bread. And, of course, a bottle of wine, some more of the vineyard's dry rosé, which would pair well with the food and be refreshing on a warm day.

Bailey watched as he set out everything. "You definitely planned ahead, didn't you? This looks great."

"I hope you'll like it."

Her eyes met his, warm, approving. "So far I've liked pretty much everything you've done for me."

She was so close, her mouth so inviting. Nasim bent toward her, kissed her, tasted her. They bent toward one another—but then she pulled back slightly with a shake of her head.

"If we keep going, we're going to crush all this food."

That was true. Well, they could hold the thought and follow up later.

"You're right. We should eat, I suppose."

The sunlight danced in her blue eyes as she grinned at him. "That is why we came out here, right?"

"Right," he said, although the word sounded somewhat strangled even to him. In that particular moment, he was questioning his decision to hold off on any more intimacies until after they'd eaten. His body throbbed with need for her, and suddenly the multiple times they'd made love the night before seemed as if they'd happened a very long time ago. He cleared his throat. "Let me pour you some wine."

Bailey only nodded, remaining silent as he uncorked the rosé and filled both their glasses. After he was done and had set the bottle back in the picnic basket, she raised her glass and said, "To a sunny day."

He could definitely drink to that. And he knew it was all the sunnier because she was in it.

They drank, and were quiet for a time as they sampled the food on the platter. When they spoke again, it was of inconsequential enough matters— how he had found this estate while familiarizing himself with the winery's surroundings, how he'd begun studying winemaking over the winter when he had little else to do with his time. Bailey talked a little of the strategies she'd used during that same time, staying alive while the djinn hunted her in downtown Los Angeles.

"I fear my winter was more happily spent than yours," Nasim said as he poured them some more wine.

That comment elicited a resigned lift of her shoulders. "Maybe. But…it was kind of exciting at the same time. At least I wasn't bored very often."

No, he supposed she wasn't. It would be hard to be bored when at any moment you could find yourself pursued by implacable foes.

He watched her as she reached over and picked up a small square of white cheddar and popped it in her mouth. As soon as they'd gotten out of the car, she'd removed the scarf, and her hair lay on her shoulders like a glory of scattered sunshine.

In that moment, he felt a rush of affection so strong, it almost took his breath away. He wanted things to remain as they were now—with him and Bailey together, enjoying the beauty of this land that was his new home. He wanted it to be her home as well, now and forever. Why should he fight against this attraction, one that had become love so subtly, he was not even sure when it happened?

Certainly after making love to her the night

before, he knew he never wanted to hold another woman in his arms.

Somehow sensing his regard, she looked over at him, expression suddenly puzzled, and perhaps a little wary. "What is it?"

"I was just thinking."

Mouth quirking, she said, "That can be dangerous."

More than you know, he thought. Voice quiet, he told her, "I want you to be my Chosen."

All of a sudden, Bailey went still, like a wild animal that had suddenly realized it had been spotted by a hunter. "We've already talked about this," she said, her tone flat.

"A little. Not enough."

She was silent for a moment. "I don't know what more there is to discuss. It's crazy to think that we could commit to something like that when we hardly know each other."

"We've spent almost a week constantly in one another's company. I wouldn't say that is 'hardly knowing each other.'"

Another pause. Her fingers plucked at the heavy cloth on which they sat. "Nasim...this is a lot to ask of me."

"Is it?" When she didn't reply at once, he went on, "Just now, when I tried to think of letting you just walk away...I couldn't. I don't want that day to come—and it needn't come. Not if you agree to be my Chosen. Of course I cannot force you to do such a thing. But please, think about it before you say anything else."

Abruptly, she pushed herself up from the picnic blanket and walked a few paces away, stood by the water's edge, and looked out across the lake. The wind caught at her hair, making it shimmer in the sunlight like strands of the purest gold.

Somehow, Nasim knew he should remain where he was. He needed to give her what little space he could, so she might think over his proposition. If she said no—

His breath caught at the thought of losing her, but he knew he would make himself abide by her decision. More than that, he would see her safely to Los Alamos, if that was what she wished. He owed her that, for the gift she had given him of her affection, even if she did not envision that affection lasting forever.

Time passed, perhaps a few minutes, perhaps many more. He was so tense that he hadn't allowed himself to look upward at the sky, to gauge the passing of the sun. At last she turned back around toward him. Her features were quite still, and so he couldn't begin to guess what might be going through her mind right then.

Then she took a step forward, and another, and another, and suddenly she was in his arms, kissing him, her fingers tangling in his hair. When at last they pulled apart, she looked up into his eyes, the most beautiful smile he'd ever seen touching her lips.

"Yes," she said. "Mostly because I kept trying to imagine what my life would be like without you, and I couldn't. I don't want to go to New Mexico. California is my home…and now you're my home, too."

"As you are mine," Nasim replied. He drew in a breath, then said the words that would make her his forever. "Bailey O'Keefe, you are my Chosen, and my protection is given to you."

"So formal," she remarked, eyes dancing.

"I had to state my intention to the universe," he told her. "But now, I would very much like to take you to our home."

"Good," she said. "Because I want to make sure you prove to me how much you need me."

He matched her grin with one of his own. "That, my dear, will not be at all difficult."

SIXTEEN

THIS WAS PROBABLY CRAZY. NO, BAILEY KNEW it was *definitely* crazy, and yet she couldn't quite keep herself from feeling deliriously happy at what had just transpired. She wouldn't have to say goodbye to Nasim. They could be together forever.

Put that way, the whole prospect seemed a little daunting. But she didn't have to think in terms of forever. She could think of days like the one they shared now, enjoying one another's company, planning meals, driving and exploring and learning what it meant to take care of the gorgeous property that had been given to him. That made everything feel much more manageable.

They finished their picnic meal, toasting one another with rosé, trading bite-sized pieces of cheese and meat, popping grapes into each other's mouths. Maybe they were being silly, but no one was around to see, so why not? Frankly, after all she'd suffered and seen since the Heat swept over the world, she thought she could use a little silliness.

At last, though, they were done, and packed up the remains of the late lunch and headed back to the car. As promised, Bailey handed over the key fob to Nasim.

"Here you go," she said. "It's a nice little ride."

"But you prefer your Porsche," he replied, eyes crinkling a bit at the corners as he smiled.

"I do. Can you blame me?"

"Not really, except that it's not a convertible."

She had to admit that even a sunroof wasn't a replacement for a true convertible top. "Well, it's not like I'm asking you to get rid of this car. But if you could bring my Porsche up here—"

"Of course," Nasim said, although there was a certain hesitation right before he replied, one she couldn't quite figure out.

"That won't be a problem, will it?"

"No. Luckily, there's all that covered parking behind the chateau, so we can have quite a stable if we so choose."

A stable of cars. Bailey had read about that sort of thing, but never in a million years would she have expected to end up with a baker's dozen of exotic cars to play with. Then again, she would never have expected to fall in love with a djinn, either.

Sometimes life could be very strange.

They got in their red convertible, and Bailey took her scarf, which she'd tied around her wrist for safekeeping, and pulled it over her head, tying the ends under her hair. Afterward, she settled back against the seat and watched as Nasim turned the car around and pointed it back toward the Montelena estate.

It was fun to watch him drive, watch the wind catch in his hair. His profile was fine and sharp against the backdrop of passing trees. Right now he wasn't driving with any particular haste, letting the car dictate their speed. One hand was on the steering wheel, the other resting on the gearshift, even though the Spider was an automatic and he really didn't need to do any shifting. That was all right; she still liked looking at those hands, at his tanned skin and strong fingers. She recalled how those fingers had touched her, stroked her, the night before, and a rush of heat went through her body. Right now she was feeling pleasantly buzzed and not too full, and she thought it would be nice if they went back and spent the rest of the afternoon in leisurely lovemaking.

Love. It was all right to let that word echo in her mind, color all her interactions with the man who drove the little sports car so expertly. She loved him. No more hiding behind weak phrases like "having feelings for" or "caring about." Bailey loved Nasim, full stop. And that was a miracle in itself.

He lifted his right hand from the gearshift and laid it on top of her left where it rested on the seat. "You're happy with this?"

"Very happy," she replied. In fact, she was fairly certain she'd never been quite this happy, or this relaxed. It was as though she'd acknowledged what fate had planned for her and was willing to go with it. That wasn't very much like the old Bailey, but it was possible that she could only have gotten to this place by making her way through all the troubles and trials that had brought her here. "In fact, once we get home, I'm going to show you exactly how happy it's made me."

He grinned, although he kept his eyes on the road, since they were now traveling through a particularly winding section of the rural highway. "I think that sounds like a wonderful idea."

Good to know they were on the same page. She adjusted her scarf, which had begun to slip backward on her head, and watched the trees as they flashed by, at secret little lanes and roads that led off to who knows where. At some point, she'd find out, she supposed; it would be good to explore the area even more, although it looked like it might be a good idea to use a four-wheel-drive vehicle on some of those tracks.

Not that that would be a problem. Nasim could just summon them a Jeep or a Range Rover to add to their planned "stable" of vehicles.

They turned down the lane that led to the winery. As they came around the final curve and the chateau was clearly visible at last, she realized someone was standing in front of the large, arched door of the lower-level entrance. A tall someone, wearing djinn robes all in black.

At once, Nasim tensed, and she thought she heard him mutter, "Damn it," under his breath.

"Who is that?" she asked, body already flooding with fight-or-flight hormones. Her right hand rested on the door handle, even though they hadn't come to a stop yet. "Have the reavers found us?"

"No," he replied at once. He slowed and brought the car to a halt. "That's Idris, one of the elders."

Well, that wasn't so bad. He'd probably come here to read Nasim the riot act about being shacked up with a human, but since she was now his Chosen, this Idris was going to find out that he'd come all the way out here for nothing.

The elder didn't come to the car, but waited for Nasim and Bailey to get out and approach the front door of the chateau. As she drew closer,

Bailey could see that this djinn might have been an elder, but he didn't look all that old, maybe in his early thirties at the most. He was handsome like all djinn, with black hair that fell to his shoulders and dark eyes to match.

Those eyes narrowed slightly as Bailey and Nasim came to stand a foot or so away from them. However, he didn't get the chance to speak first, because Nasim jumped right in, saying, "Well met, Idris. What can we do for you today?"

Idris' mouth compressed slightly. When he spoke, his voice was deep and smooth, although Bailey thought she could still detect a note of annoyance in it. "It is more what you can do for me, Nasim al-Jibril. Would you like to explain why you have brought this mortal woman to your estate?"

"Of course," Nasim replied. He was smiling and seemed at ease despite their unexpected visitor, but Bailey was standing close enough to know that he was not as relaxed as he wanted those around him to believe. There was a certain tension in his body that she couldn't quite explain. After all, she was his Chosen now, so everything should be kosher, right? "This is Bailey O'Keefe, and she has just agreed to become my Chosen."

"Congratulations," Idris said. "I am glad to hear it." There was nothing in his tone or his expression to indicate that he was particularly happy for them, though. He went on, "I am glad I will not have to chastise you on that particular topic, Nasim, but you know you cannot remain here with her."

What? Bailey glanced up at Nasim, saw worry but no real surprise in his expression. Crossing her arms, she said, "Why can't we stay here? These are his lands, aren't they?"

The elder's gaze flicked to her for a second, then returned to Nasim. "You have not explained this to her?"

"No, I hadn't yet had the opportunity to tell her all the ramifications of becoming my partner. She only agreed to become my Chosen this afternoon."

"What haven't you explained?" Bailey demanded, hands on her hips. Clearly, Nasim had been keeping something from her, and she wasn't too happy about that at the moment. However, she also knew it was probably not a good idea to start arguing in front of Idris. As hard as it was, she made herself wait for him to explain his reasoning.

It was Idris who replied, though. "Djinn and their Chosen live apart from the rest of our people, in their own settlements. The one nearest here is in Monterey, but it's not required that you go there, only that you join one of the California communities."

She stared at him, irritation surging through her. Not that she had anything against Monterey—she'd never even been there—but the mere fact that this high-and-mighty elder was dictating where she and Nasim could live really chapped her ass. "Why?"

Idris frowned, but it was Nasim who replied. "Because that's what was agreed upon. There were a lot of djinn who wanted all of humanity wiped out, but those who had selected Chosen said they would live apart so the rest of the djinn wouldn't have to have anything to do with them."

"Nice of you to tell me about this," she snapped, knowing she was already ignoring her own advice to herself to keep calm.

"I would have," he said, his tone placating. "I simply hadn't gotten around to it."

"You know now," Idris put in. "And that means you must make plans to leave this place."

"What if I don't want to?"

Nasim put a hand on her arm. "Bailey—"

She didn't pull her arm from his grasp, but she did ignore his plea. "No, Nasim. I want Idris to tell me exactly why we can't stay in the home that he and the other two elders gave you in the first place."

The elder frowned down at her. He was very tall, taller even than Nasim. "Because, as your lover has told you, that is what was agreed upon."

There was nothing she hated more than being told something had always been done a particular way, as if precedent was the be-all, end-all of the universe. "Well, *I* didn't agree to it. Who's going to take care of the vines here?"

"That is none of your concern."

"Actually, it is. If you djinn keep guzzling wine at anything close to the rate I've seen Nasim drink it, the world is going to be facing a real shortage not too far off. And if no one's making any new wine, what then?"

It could have been a trick of the sunlight, the way it danced its way across the leaves of the trees that surrounded the chateau, but Bailey almost thought she saw Idris' mouth quirk. "Yours is not the only vineyard that was given over to a djinn's care."

"Still," she said. "What's the harm in our staying here? And don't say it's not safe or some other bullshit—I know Nasim can protect the two of us just fine."

"Bailey—" Now Nasim's expression truly was strained. He probably couldn't believe she was talking to one of the elders that way, but right then, she just didn't care. She'd allowed herself to start thinking of the vineyard as home, to start wondering about what her life here would be like, and she was damned if some goddamn djinn elder was going to pop in from nowhere and start dictating where she was able to live.

"That is part of the reason," Idris said. "While the punishment for raising a hand against a djinn's Chosen is a severe one, I can't promise you that someone might not try, once they know the two of you are living here alone without a community's protection."

"You can't promise that someone will, either," she countered. "It seems stupid to make us leave all this, just on the off chance that some rogue djinn will get a bee up his ass and come here to make trouble."

Yes, that was definitely a smile on the elder's wide, somehow sensual mouth. His gaze moved to Nasim. "Your Chosen has a…colorful turn of phrase."

Which she supposed was the polite way of saying she didn't appear to give a damn who she was talking to.

Nasim smiled as well, if a little ruefully. "She is a woman who speaks her mind, and I love her for it."

Was it fair for such a simple comment to make her feel as if she was melting inside? Her irritation vanished, replaced by her own love for this man, this djinn, who obviously didn't feel there was any need to make excuses for her, no matter how she should have been speaking to an elder.

She reached over and took Nasim's hand, felt his strong fingers clamp around hers. "Yes, I'm speaking my mind. You've given me excuses, but not a lot of real reasons. Who cares if Nasim and I live here together on our own? We're not hurting anyone. We'll actually be doing some good."

Once again, Idris' lips twitched. "There are vineyards outside Monterey, you know."

"But they're not *this* vineyard."

"No, they are not." The elder paused and turned slightly so he could survey the impressive stone building behind him. "It is rather a magnificent place, I will grant you that."

"Well, then," Nasim put in. "You know that Bailey has the right of it. We will not come to any harm here. The world is wide, and this is only a very small corner of it. No one will come looking for us in this place."

"You can't know that for certain."

"It's a risk we're willing to take." Nasim looked down at her, his fingers giving hers a reassuring squeeze. "Aren't we?"

"Yes," she said firmly, staring straight at Idris. "Not that I think it's much of a risk."

The elder shrugged, the black silk of his robes glinting in the bright sun. "Very well. I suppose I shall think of some way to explain this to Ibram and Istar."

Nasim's brows pulled together. It seemed pretty obvious that he wasn't too thrilled by Idris' comment. "They will not attempt to overrule your decision, will they?"

A dart of fear went through Bailey. She hadn't even thought of that. Did Idris even have the authority to make a unilateral decision about her and Nasim's fate?

"No," Idris replied, and at once Bailey relaxed a little. "They will trust my judgment in this matter." His dark gaze swept over the two of them, and he added, "Do not make that judgment a mistake."

Before they could reply, he had disappeared, making that odd little *pop* which always seemed to accompany a djinn's departure. For a second, Bailey could only stare at the place where Idris had stood. Had he really just said it was okay for her and Nasim to stay here?

"I am sorry, Bailey," Nasim said. To be fair, he really did look contrite. "I was going to explain all that to you. I just thought we would have more time."

"It's all right," she replied. She shifted so she faced him, and then reached out to take his other hand, now holding both of them, fingers entwined. "I mean, it all worked out in the end."

"I suppose it did." He looked away from her, his glance seeming to take in their surroundings. "And you're not worried about staying here without any other djinn around to protect us?"

"Of course I'm not worried." That was only the truth; as he'd told Idris, the world was a big place, and she doubted any other djinn would expend the effort to track them down here, especially when the punishment for doing so sounded as though it would be very unpleasant. "Are you?"

"Not at all," he said, so quickly that she knew he was telling her the truth. "I am sure we'll be left here in peace."

"Good." This little run-in with Idris had only postponed the rest of the afternoon's activities; now that Bailey knew they would be safe, would be left alone, she wanted to seal this whole Chosen deal with Nasim. Yes, he'd said those formal words back by the lake, had said announcing his intentions was all he needed to do, but she was thinking of something a little more physical. "That means you can blink us up to your bedroom so we can work off some of that lunch."

He didn't reply, only pulled her to him, kissing her, tongue exploring her mouth. In the next instant, they were upstairs on the bed, articles of clothing being thrown this way and that, all those barriers tossed aside so their bodies could meet once again a rush of sex that was fast and furious and hard and exactly what she needed right then. She clung to him, shuddering with climax, felt him come as well. Yes, that was it.

They truly had sealed the deal.

Afterward, they lay in bed, holding one another, his fingers playing absently with her loose hair. All of a sudden, though, he sat up and stared down at her as a wicked grin played around the corners of his mouth.

"That was amazing, my love," he said. "But I was thinking of something else we could do."

"What?" Bailey asked, pushing herself up from the pillows. When Nasim smiled like that, you knew he was up to something.

Out of nowhere, a pair of key fobs appeared on his outstretched hand. Still grinning, he asked,

"Want to race?"

The End

THE WITCHES OF CANYON ROAD

(Paranormal Romance)

Hidden Gifts

Darker Paths

Mysterious Ways

A Canyon Road Christmas (November 2018)

Demon Born (January 2019)

―――

DJINN DOMINION*

(Paranormal Romance)

Stolen

Forgotten

Driven

―――

THE WITCHES OF CLEOPATRA HILL*

(Paranormal Romance)

Darkangel

Darknight

Darkmoon

Sympathetic Magic

Protector

Spellbound

A Cleopatra Hill Christmas

Impractical Magic

Strange Magic

The Arrangement

Defender

Bad Blood

Deep Magic

Darktide

THE DJINN WARS*

(Paranormal Romance)

Chosen

Taken

Fallen

Broken

Forsaken

Forbidden

Awoken

Illuminated

THE WATCHERS TRILOGY*

(Paranormal Romance)

Falling Dark

Dead of Night

Rising Dawn

THE SEDONA FILES*

(Paranormal Romance)

Bad Vibrations

Desert Hearts

Angel Fire

Star Crossed

Falling Angels

Enemy Mine

TALES OF THE LATTER KINGDOMS

(Fantasy Romance)

All Fall Down

Dragon Rose

Binding Spell

Ashes of Roses

One Thousand Nights

Threads of Gold

The Wolf of Harrow Hall

Moon Dance

The Song of the Thrush

Snow Fall (first half of 2019)

———

THE GAIAN CONSORTIUM SERIES

(Science Fiction Romance)

Blood Will Tell

Breath of Life

The Gaia Gambit

The Mandala Maneuver

The Titan Trap

The Zhore Deception

Refugees (October 2018)

* Indicates a completed series

ABOUT THE AUTHOR

USA Today bestselling author Christine Pope has been writing stories ever since she commandeered her family's Smith-Corona typewriter back in grade school. Her work includes paranormal romance, fantasy romance, and science fiction/space opera romance. She makes her home in Sedona, Arizona.

Don't miss out on any of Christine's new releases —sign up for her newsletter today!

Christine Pope on the Web:
www.christinepope.com